HEADLESS

BY REG IVORY

iUniverse, Inc.
Bloomington

HEADLESS

iUniverse books may be ordered through booksellers or by contacting:

iUniverse
1663 Liberty Drive
Bloomington, IN 47403
www.iuniverse.com
1-800-Authors (1-800-288-4677)

ISBN: 978-1-4759-8765-2 (sc)
ISBN: 978-1-4759-8767-6 (hc)
ISBN: 978-1-4759-8766-9 (e)

Library of Congress Control Number: 2013907568

Printed in the United States of America.

iUniverse rev. date: 5/9/2013

To the men of the B-52 crews, past and present—my brothers.

She was perfect—a tall, slim redhead with a mouth that looked like Leonardo had found a way to improve the Mona Lisa. Green eyes, with maybe a far-off Latin hint, flawless skin. She looked about twenty-five or so and wore the casual but elegant tennis outfit that was almost a requirement for Roswell housewives. It had a classic new look on her. Diamonds circled her lovely neck. A very expensive emerald tennis bracelet was hard to miss too. All in all, a fine package. You could tell she was used to being admired, but it didn't seem to affect her. I saw her give me a quick appraisal and remain unimpressed. She was confident, not arrogant. She moved up to my desk and held out her hand.

"Mr. Novak? My name is Carol Chambers. I called earlier."

I stood and held her hand for as long as I could without seeming obvious. I failed.

"Yes. Please sit down."

She moved easily into a chair. "It was nice of you to see me. Roxanne Roden recommended you. Said you were a discreet detective and ..." She paused, smiling. "And wholesomely aggressive."

Roxanne had been a frequent sexual partner several years ago when we started seeing each other; she'd been in between husbands. I bailed her out of a blackmail jam, and she made it worth my while. In a lot of ways. We'd certainly been aggressive with each other; neither one of us wanted anything wholesome. Whatever else this Chambers woman was, her friendship with Roxanne meant she ran in rich-bitch circles. Roxie was a very clever woman who used men, drugs, and other women, sometimes simultaneously. I wondered what else she had told Carol Chambers about me: that I was a man who shunned commitments like

1

the plague; an alcoholic; late thirties and looking older; obnoxious about his fondness for Bobby Darin? At least I was kind to cats.

"And how is the lovely Roxanne?" I said.

"She's still lovely. Remarried now."

"That's good to hear." I didn't care about her marriage, but it was conversation. "And what can I do for you, Mrs. Chambers?"

She stared at me for a moment. "I thought my last name might—well, I suppose Chambers isn't all that unique." She took a deep breath. "Do you recall the news story about my husband Don's death—murder— about two years ago here in Roswell? The body was found on Vintage Road." It was obviously difficult for her to talk about.

I did remember it—very well. Anyone in our area of Atlanta would have. It was a gruesome story and had a big play in the papers and on television for almost six months. Donald Chambers's headless body had been found in the woods off Vintage. He had been there about a week. His body was covered with at least a dozen deep knife wounds. The fingerprints weren't too far gone for an ID. His wallet and a few hundred bucks were intact, so probably not a robbery. There was speculation about a drug deal gone wrong, and the police hinted at some deviant sexual involvement that was never explained. He was a wealthy Delta pilot, well known. The whole thing was the talk of the Roswell tennis set for months. And the cops never found his head.

"Yes. I do remember. I'm sorry for your loss."

She nodded. "Thank you. I'm sure you can tell I'm not close to being over it. It's hard to bring it all back." She was either a great actress or really feeling it.

"I understand. I'm assuming the police have never found the murderer or we would have read about it."

"That's correct. There's hasn't been a word from them in almost two years. Frankly, I don't think they've ever really pursued the case." Her lovely mouth was grim as she touched her diamond necklace.

I wanted a cigarette but was into my third week after quitting cold turkey, and I ignored the craving for a while. I wanted a drink, too, but then again, I always wanted a drink. "I was a Roswell cop for two years. There are some good ones and others who are just putting in time, waiting to retire."

"Yes, I guess I had more of the latter."

"Mrs. Chambers, I don't know how I can help you after all this time. The police may have been slow, but they have access to many more avenues of research and investigation than I do. I'm sure they've covered every lead. How can I help?" I knew this was a cold, dead case, but it was worth watching her while she talked.

"There are things—things I never told the police. Things that may help."

"And why didn't you tell the police?"

"Donald—Don—told me—that is, he asked me ..." She stopped and folded her hands in her lap and looked up, trying hard to control herself. "This is where the discreet part comes in, Mr. Novak."

"Please call me Jack."

Another deep breath. "I met Don about five years ago. He was flying for Delta. He was older—thirty years older than I was—divorced, a genuinely nice guy." She looked up, staring directly at me. "I hadn't met many men like Don in my life."

"Go on."

"The truth is, I was—I was working for an escort service in Houston. I made good money and really didn't care where my life was going. There were lots of men, drugs, and—other things. I was at a Delta Airlines party and happened to meet Don." Tears shone in her eyes. "The short story is—he changed my life."

"How so?"

She looked past my head, toward the ceiling. "Don accepted me as I was despite my ... background and previous lifestyle. He never asked me anything about myself, but I told him the whole story—everything. He never criticized or tried to change me. He and his son completely accepted me into their lives."

I had forgotten a son was involved. "Is his son still—does he still live at home?"

"Yes. Hank—Henry— is twenty and in his second year at Georgia now. He still comes home on weekends."

With a stepmother who looked like this, I wondered why he ever left for college. "Mrs. Chambers, I have to ask. Was there—is there—anything ...?"

"You want to know if Hank and I ever had a relationship. The answer is no. The police pursued that avenue for several weeks, along with other accusations I resented." She sounded bitter.

"It's an obvious angle in a murder case like this, especially when your ages are so close."

"I would never have done anything like that to Don—even after he was ... gone. Besides, Hank and I are just good friends."

I wondered just how good as I admired her body once again. "Mrs. Chambers, exactly what is it you'd be expecting me to do for you?"

"I want you to find my husband's murderer, or murderers. I don't care how long it takes." She paused and looked down at her folded hands. "And there's something else."

I waited, still wanting a cigarette.

"My husband was a B-52 pilot in Vietnam. Flew over two hundred missions, including the Hanoi bombings. He was very proud of his service."

"That's admirable, but I don't see how it—"

"Part of the time he was stationed at a small B-52 base in Thailand, on the Gulf."

"Yes, Utapao. I heard about it from some of the old timers when I was in the service."

"That's right. Toward the end of Vietnam, Don and his crew—they were very close—came into possession of a large number of precious stones." Again, she reached up to touch the diamonds at her throat. "Rubies and sapphires from a remote mine somewhere on the Thai border, he said."

That did it. She had me. The way she looked was enough, but the precious stones angle made her impossible to resist.

"What do you mean by 'came into possession,' Mrs. Chambers?"

"Don was reluctant to explain. I guessed it wasn't exactly legal." She paused again. "He told me some people were killed."

"Any idea how much the stones are worth?"

She stared at me for a moment. "Don said several million."

I doubted that. "Uncut stones are hard to value. How did he come up with that figure?"

"Don took them to a friend, an American appraiser retired in

Bangkok—someone he had flown with and trusted. He said he only showed the man a few jewels, telling him he found them along the Thai coast. Evidently the man was quite impressed and gave him an estimated value. He said they were of a very high quality. Don got a more recent appraisal from a reputable man in Hong Kong, who valued them even higher. I don't know how many stones actually exist, but Don led me to believe there were quite a few. He did the math and came up with an approximate value."

"And who knows about all this?"

"His crew, of course, but four of them are dead now. A B-52 has six crew members. Me. And Hank."

"Anyone else?"

She sighed. "Right before Don was murdered, he told me some Asian men had been following him. He was sure they were after the gems." This time she put her hands to her face. "I think they murdered Don for the jewels. I never told any of this to the police."

It was my turn to take a deep breath. "And where are the gems?"

"I don't know. Don was the only one who knew. He said he had hidden them somewhere in the area. He left some papers he said were clues in our safe at home. I've looked at them, but they mean nothing to me. The notes appear to be written in some Asian language."

"Mrs. Chambers, there are a couple of things that don't make sense to me. First, it's been more than thirty years since the end of the Vietnam War. Why didn't your husband do something about the gems for all that time?"

"He said he tried to sell them several times over the years but there were complications. He and most of his crew were still in the air force for several years after Vietnam and wanted to stay until retirement. And there was a formal investigation—because of the deaths in Thailand. Don and his crew were never charged, but they were under suspicion for some time."

"But surely the crew must have wanted some money out of this before now?"

"As I said, four of them have passed away. A few were fairly well off. Don was actually quite wealthy himself. He had inherited some substantial family money, plus his air force retirement and a good job with Delta. Part of the problem was the fear that doing something with the gems might trigger the old investigation. As I said, some people had been killed."

"And his crew was okay with this?"

"Yes. They agreed to let Don handle it when he thought the time was right. If any of them needed money, they came to Don. He was always very generous. You have to understand that the crew was fiercely loyal; Don had been their commander. He kept them safe through many tough missions. They were almost killed over Hanoi. But he was getting ready to do something with the gems when—"

"Is it possible the remaining crew members are involved in his death?"

"I can't imagine that could be true. I've met them. Some of them have been to our home. I never sensed any problems or disagreements."

"You said that no one else knew about the gems, but you also said there had been an investigation—by the air force."

"Yes."

"So could anyone from the air force be involved in this—in his murder—because of the gems?"

Her eyes widened slowly. "I never considered that. I suppose it's possible."

I shook my head. "Mrs. Chambers, I'm sorry, but this is a lot bigger situation than I usually handle. I do divorces and blackmails and political crap. Murders and Asians and gemstones are more than a little out of my league. My advice is to go to the police and tell them what you've told me."

She frowned. "What good would that do? They accomplished nothing the first time. And I don't want the publicity starting up again. Please. Please at least try. I know how difficult this is, and I'm not expecting miracles. Those gems are mine now and I want them, dammit. You don't know—it's been so hard with Don gone. I get these feelings …" Suddenly she stopped and smiled strangely at me; she crossed her legs slowly. "In addition to your usual fees, we can come to some agreement about the gems, if you find them. Call it a commission. Perhaps twenty percent of their value?" She leaned slightly toward me. "And call me Carol."

As if millions of dollars in gems weren't enough, she definitely knew how to motivate men. Especially men like me. Our mutual friend Roxanne must have tipped her off. Roxie got high on whatever the drug of the month was. I got high on women. And Jameson. And I hadn't gotten high in quite a while. I kept staring at her mouth. And her legs. It was easy to make up my mind. Besides, I had nothing else going on.

"Let's do this, Mrs. Cham—Carol. I'll give it two weeks. My fee is $250 a day plus expenses. At the end of that time, we can assess where we are and whether or not it makes sense to keep going. If we do continue and I locate the gems, we can discuss a further commission. Is that satisfactory?"

She smiled as if she knew she had me. She was right.

"That's fine. Thank you."

"In the meantime, please make me a list of people who were close friends of your husband's, both here in Roswell and others from the service that you may know about. I'll need addresses and phone numbers if you have them. I'm especially interested in his former crew members, of course."

"I'll have the list tonight. If you'll stop by the house, you can pick it up, along with a check. Say about eight?"

She reached out for my hand, and this time she let me hold it as long as I wanted.

Roswell police headquarters were only a couple of miles from my office. With the traffic the way it was—always bad—I could have walked there faster than I drove it. The building hadn't changed a bit. Square, gray, three stories, flag at the entrance. The architecture had no imagination at all. Neither did most of the cops. For a while it had been home. And there were still a few good friends.

Sgt. Homer Kenney, with the inevitable nickname of "Homes," was in his office, a pile of papers centered before him and a large cup of coffee beside the pile. Homes had been my training officer during my ninety-day rookie break-in period, and we hit it off. Turned out we had a lot in common. He liked the ladies, the Braves, and beer. We kept the friendship going after I left and had shared some tough times together. Homes was the only cop in Roswell who had been shot three times in the line of duty. He claimed one of them was because of a jealous husband, but we all knew better. I would trust him with anything. Now he handled some cold cases but was still active on the street. He was also one of the most respected officers on the force and knew everyone in town. I knocked on the open door. "Hey, Homes."

"Jack, my favorite alcoholic. How's the private peeper business? Have a seat." He looked grayer and heavier. Must be fifty now.

"Fair, Homes. Just fair. I need a favor."

He smiled and tilted his chair back. "I ought to get a ten-percent cut of your business, but I'd take a ten-percent cut of your women."

I laughed. "You'd come out on the short end either way. But I do have kind of a woman problem."

"Your only problem is listening to that goddamned Bobby Darin all the time. It's poisoned your mind. Probably why you drink so damned much." He gave me that straight-on, no-shit look he had. "And how's that going, by the way—the drinking?"

I grinned at him. "Not a drop in nineteen months and seven days."

"Sounds like you might have it licked, buddy."

"No way, Homes. I can feel it every day. Every hour."

He straightened his chair and took a sip of coffee. "Well, how about some coffee? Want a cup?"

"No thanks. You're probably still reheating the stuff you made two years ago. Homes, you got anything I can see on the Chambers murder from a few years back?"

His eyes widened a little. "You mean the headless guy we found out in the woods? The one with the hooker wife?"

"Yeah, that's the one. Why do you call her a hooker?"

He sighed and smiled. "Jesus, Jack, don't tell me you're dating the Chambers broad. Aren't you ever attracted to any normal women? There's that Darin influence again. Christ, listen to some Sinatra, for God's sake."

"Yeah, like Sinatra was attracted to normal women. Carol Chambers looks pretty normal to me, Homes. Super-normal. Perfect, maybe." I winked back at him.

"Well, I'll give you that. She's a babe, for sure." He got up from his desk and walked to a series of file cabinets along the wall. He opened one, flipped through some tabs, and finally pulled one out.

"It goes without saying that I'm not supposed to do this, right?" He handed me the file.

"Right. I'll just sit here and look through it; maybe make some notes. Unless I'm keeping you from something?"

"Yeah, sure. From what? Take your time."

I looked at the photographs first. They were incredibly gory. Most of them hadn't appeared in the *Atlanta Constitution* or on television, for obvious reasons. The next thing that grabbed my attention was a copy of a rap sheet from the Houston PD on Carol Cleveland before she married Don Chambers. She had a couple of arrests for solicitation and some minor drug busts that were pled out. Never served any time. Even in her police mug shots she looked good. A lot better now.

"Told you she was a hooker," Homes said. "And a druggie."

"I didn't see any evidence of that this morning in my office."

"So she's really your client?"

"Looks like it. She wants me to find out who murdered her husband." I said nothing about the gems. Then I saw another photo of the headless body. It was indeed covered with stab wounds. There were also several strange symbols and what appeared to be Asian writing on the torso, apparently applied with something like a small paint brush or perhaps a permanent marker.

"Homes, what's this Chinese stuff on his body? I never read about that in the papers."

"Naw, we held that back in case we got a break. And it ain't Chinese. The Asian Studies guy from Kennesaw State says they're cult symbols. Maybe some religious shit. He said the language was probably Cambodian. Maybe some Japanese thrown in. Who the hell can figure those people out, anyway? We thought Chambers was into some drug deals, which may have included his wife. The guy was a Delta pilot and flew all over Asia. He could have made the contacts."

"Ever prove any of that?"

"Nope. We couldn't find out shit. The wife didn't talk much, although I interviewed her several times." He smiled. "A couple of times for no real reason. Then we found out about the kid and thought we were on to something."

"That's Henry?"

"Hank—yeah. Goes to school at Georgia, I think. He's had a little problem with drugs up there, too, but who the hell hasn't in college nowadays."

I looked at the copy of the kid's sheet from the Clarke County police. A minor bust for pot and some pills. He paid a fine and did some community service. There was nothing else.

"You said you were on to something?"

"Yeah. When you start adding up the drug stuff, the fact that the guy was a pilot, the Cambodian shit on his body, the former hooker wife, and the kid—we thought we had a case developing. But we could never pull it all together." He took another sip of coffee. "I'll tell you something else, though, Jack. Houston PD said she was into some very kinky stuff over there. And the lovely Mrs. Chambers is hooked up with a fast crowd right here in Roswell. And if that chick and her stepson ain't getting it on, I can't smell it as good as I used to."

I finished making notes and flipping through the file and handed it back to him. I saw no mention of jewels. "I asked her about that; she denies it. By the way, can I get you to e-mail me copies of these photos?"

"Sure. Oh—one of those times I went out to interview her—unannounced—I saw her and the kid through one of the front windows as I walked up to the house—the mansion, I should say. They live in Camelot."

"And what did you see, my friend? Tell me slowly and in great detail." We both laughed.

"They were wrapped around each other pretty tight. I never hugged my momma like that."

"Technically, she isn't his momma."

"True. But his dad—her husband—hadn't been dead for a month. They looked hotter than hell to me. So I just drove away." He smiled again.

"Watching dogs do it in the park used to make you pretty hot, you old bastard."

He grinned, scratching his beard. "Look, Jack, I know what you've got on your mind. She was on my mind, too, for quite a while after the case went cold. She's probably good for some fun for a while. But you ain't gonna find out what's behind those lovely green eyes. She's covering up a lot of shit, and I never could figure it out. Cool on the outside, boiling on the inside. There's plenty she wasn't telling us. I know she's got tons of money—he had family bucks and lots of insurance—so maybe you should jack up your fees."

I smiled and stood up. "Maybe I should. Or maybe I'll just take it out in trade."

"Sounds like the old Jack," Homes said. "I'd watch out for the kid, though. He was very protective of his momma—his step-momma—when I talked to the two of them together. He's a big guy, and I don't think he'd like any competition."

"I'll keep that in mind. Thanks, Homes. You know anybody in

Houston PD I can talk to in case I want to dig deeper into the Chambers woman's background?

"Yeah. Call Billy Busbin." Homes opened a card file in a desk drawer and handed me one. "Billy sent me her rap sheet. Just tell him you and I are buds."

"Thanks. How about we meet at TJ's and have a few drinks?"

"You're not goin' off the wagon, are you buddy?"

"Not yet. But you know I like to hang out."

"Okay. Sounds good. That waitress still there? What was her name?"

"Rhiannon. Like the old Fleetwood Mac song."

"Right. How about Friday at six?"

"See you there. And thanks a lot."

"Sure. Any time. Hey, did you see Richie Brooks outside when you came in?"

"No. Over in the park?"

"Yeah. He was asking for you the other day." Homes grinned. "You been missing those AA meetings again?"

"Regularly."

"Why don't you talk to him? He's got some new pictures." That made us both laugh.

Richie Brooks was a cross between an eccentric and a musical genius. He sat in the park across from the station and alternately played his guitar or took pictures of things that interested him. We met at an AA meeting. One night he called me from jail and asked me to come down. He didn't want to call his sponsor and knew I had some cop friends. He was arrested for taking a few pretty dull pictures of his neighbor, Mrs. Henry, in the shower. Mrs. Henry was eighty-three. Richie said the water droplets running down her body looked like a miniature tsunami. Mrs. Henry wasn't amused. I went down to the jail, talked to a couple of guys, and got him released. Ever since, he called me whenever he got into another jam. I liked Richie. He was no derelict, and we shared a love of old Negro blues.

When I left the station, I saw him in the park and waved. He waved back. I crossed the street to his bench.

"Hello, John." Richie was the only person who had ever called me John. No one could tell how old Richie was. He had a well-lined face, a long gray beard, and glasses held together with electrical tape. Fingernails so long and sharp they could cut through a steak. How the hell he could play with those things I never knew. But, man, how he could play. He was sitting on his favorite bench, guitar in his hands, camera at the ready. An old cat with one ear sat at his feet.

"Hi, Richie. Shoot any interesting neighbors lately?" It was a standard greeting.

"Now, John, you know I don't do that anymore. I take nature shots mostly and pictures of ant beds." He patted the bench next to him, and I sat down. The cat jumped up on my lap.

"Haven't seen you at any meetings lately, John."

"Haven't been to any. What's that you're playing?"

Richie knew more about playing the blues than anyone I had ever met. He found obscure music and seemed to memorize it instantly. He played well when he was sober, better when he'd had a few. Occasionally we sang together for fun.

"This is a Robert Johnson tune, "Me and the Devil Blues.""

"It's good. You play a lot of Johnson."

He nodded. "Robert knew what he was singing about." Richie played a few riffs and sang a little, giving it the feeling the song deserved.

"I like it, Rich. When are you playing at TJ's again?"

"Couple of weeks." He put the guitar down and picked up the camera. "Want to see some ants?"

"Not right now, Richie. I need to do some work. Maybe I'll see you at a meeting soon."

"Maybe don't keep you dry, John. The system keeps you dry."

I stood up and patted him on the back. "Amen to that, brother. Take care of yourself."

"I'll be praying for you, John."

"As long as you keep playing for me, Rich."

I went back to the office and looked over my notes. Then I went to the computer and typed them up in detail, along with my personal observations about the case. I knew there wasn't a chance of finding the Asian murderers—if that's who killed Don Chambers—but the gemstones intrigued me, to say nothing of the lovely widow. I called the Asian Studies department at Kennesaw State University and asked for Dr. Jack Neal. I told him I was working the Chambers case and had talked to the police. He agreed to see me the next day.

Then I called Homes's buddy Billy Busbin at the Houston PD and explained my connection to the case. We spent some time trading stories about Homes. He had some good ones I could hold over my friend's head when we got together for drinks. I asked Busbin if there was any new information about the case on his end or anything they'd turned up since the initial investigation in Roswell. He said there wasn't much but he'd e-mail me whatever he had. He laughed and said the most interesting thing they'd found was an amateur movie of Carol Cleveland with another woman. The disk had made its way around the cops at the station, as those things often did. He said he'd send it along too.

I sat there for a while thinking things through. I really felt out of my comfort zone with this Cambodian angle. Maybe the Asian professor could help me with that. I wondered if Atlanta even had a significant Asian community of any kind. It was almost six o'clock when I finished note-taking, and I figured I'd have dinner and then shower and clean up before heading to Carol Chambers's place. I didn't know what the evening might hold, but I wanted to be ready to grab onto it.

Camelot was only five miles from my apartment, but I knew it would take at least half an hour in traffic to get there. It was one of several extremely wealthy communities that had exploded east of Roswell as Atlanta and its suburbs expanded. Camelot was where most of Atlanta's professional athletes had their homes, along with a few other extravagantly wealthy people—bankers, entertainers, and some reputed drug dealers. The houses were incredible and looked like medieval castles. The cheapest place, I'd been told, went for six million, even in a lousy economy. It was where Roxanne presided over her own palace. I had been there more than once.

I drove up to the gated, guarded entrance. The man in charge was a retired Roswell cop named Don Masterson I knew a little. We traded stories for a few minutes. He showed me on a small map how to find the Chambers place. I had visited Camelot several other times, once for a New Year's party that just hadn't gone well. Everyone there but me was an athlete, and I found it difficult to watch some great players I admired drunk and high on the free-flowing booze and drugs. I drove slowly along the route on the map and admired the view. The King Arthur motif had been carried out to the last detail. The extravagant homes had parapets and medieval decorations of all kinds. Miniature broadswords and mace decorated the mailboxes and front doors, along with phony coats of arms. Friends had told me the residents often referred to each other as "Lord" and "Lady"—rich people acting stupidly. I stopped when I came to an estate with a huge boulder on the front lawn. Riveted into the face of it was a twenty-five-by-twenty-five color photo of the rap artist D-Bunk. He was twenty-two and worth over a hundred million, according to the trade papers. His mailbox was a giant gold record with another photo in the center. No problem with ego there.

I finally found the Chambers home and saw a Mercedes in the driveway that looked faintly familiar, although in Camelot there were so many I might have passed a dozen like it. I parked alongside and took in the home. More of the castle routine. It had everything but a moat around it and men on the roof with vats of boiling oil to splash down on commoners like me. When the front door opened and Carol walked toward me, I got out of my car and headed up the circular walkway. To say she looked great would have been an insult. A different tennis outfit. Different diamonds. She was cool. And stunning.

"Hi, Jack. I hope you didn't have any problem getting through the gate. We've had some burglary incidents lately, and the guards are tougher than they used to be."

I smiled, accepting her outstretched hand. "Not at all. I must still have some of my cop look."

"Come on in. An old friend of yours stopped by to say hello."

We walked into a long, vaulted entrance with what appeared to be original art along the walls. I don't know much about art but figured if the paintings weren't expensive, they wouldn't be there. As we strolled into the great room, I saw a woman at the bar with her back to us. Even from the rear, which was one of her best angles, I knew who it was. Roxanne Roden turned and did her best slow walk up to me. Her blouse and shorts were almost transparent—a typical outfit for her. She was blond for the moment. No bra and didn't need one. Roxie had plenty of good stuff and no qualms about displaying it. I wondered if she had shaved her pubic hair. Roxie had a thing about shaving just before she knew she was going to get laid. And she had worn out a hell of a lot of razors.

"Jack. It's been a long time." She put her arms around my neck, moved her body into mine the way she used to, and kissed me long and hard, as if we were alone. I could taste the gin on her lips and felt the old familiar rush immediately as I pulled her to me.

"I hate to break the two of you up." Carol was grinning. "Jack is here to do business, Roxanne."

Roxie stepped back from me and licked her lips. "You didn't say what kind of business, Carol. And I was hoping …" They both laughed.

I could barely make out Roxanne's pupils. She was high on something, but I couldn't guess what. She used a wide range of drugs with apparently no ill effects. So far. She looked great. I wondered about having the two of them together. Some old habits are hard to break.

"Jack, would you like a drink?" Carol walked over to the bar.

"Jack will have Jameson on the rocks. And you know what I want." Roxie and Carol smiled at each other, and Carol made some drink noises and motions.

"Make mine a ginger ale, please, Carol." My body was giving me signals I tried to ignore. The taste of her booze was part of it. Roxanne was the rest. Starting up with her again would be so easy. And so dangerous.

"Still being a good boy, Jackie?" Roxie smiled coyly at me.

"For the time being. I heard you got married," I said, trying to make conversation. She took a seat in a large, comfortable chair; I settled in a huge black leather sofa across from her.

"You heard right. Sam Rorscher. He's a plastic surgeon. Board certified." Roxanne accepted a glass from Carol and smiled at me as I took mine. "But he's out of town at a conference." She sipped her drink and stared at me. "For a week."

"Rorscher. At least you won't have to change the initials on your towels," I said.

"My towels don't have initials, Jack. Or don't you remember?"

Roxanne never missed a beat.

Carol chuckled as she crossed the room with an envelope and handed it to me. "You two ought to get a room."

"What's the matter with this one, honey?" Roxanne said. "I seem to recall it's seen its share of action." She stood up and moved across to sit beside me on the sofa. She put a hand on my left leg, rubbing it slowly back and forth.

I stood up and moved toward Carol. "Thanks for the information. Can I ask you a few other questions?"

"Of course." She crossed to the same sofa, sitting next to Roxie. Roxanne put an arm around Carol's shoulder.

"It's okay if we talk in front of Roxie?"

The two of them looked at each other and laughed. "Roxanne knows all my deep, dark secrets, Jack. Go ahead."

I put my drink down on a small table. "I spent some time with the Roswell police today, and they shared a little of their investigative information with me. I saw some photographs of your husband's—of your husband. I'm assuming that you saw his body at some point."

"Well, yes."

"So you're aware that there were Asian markings?"

She took a moment to reply. "Yes. I was—I didn't spend a great deal of time examining them. You can understand why."

Roxanne could never stay out of a conversation for long. "Jack, Carol's reaction was obvious. The whole thing must have been incredibly … difficult."

Difficult, I thought. Not the word I would have chosen. "Certainly. Any idea what the marks or the writing were all about?"

Carol shook her head. "I never wanted to know what they meant. I assumed they were left by the Asian men who killed him."

"If it was Asians who killed him. It could have been anyone trying to throw the police a curve."

Carol stared at her drink while Roxanne patted her on the back.

"Carol, I have an appointment in the morning with Dr. Jack Neal at Kennesaw State. He's their Asian Studies expert. He was asked by the police to study the markings. I'll see what he thinks."

Roxanne looked up at me. "I hope your appointment isn't too early."

"Early enough." I wasn't ready for Roxanne yet, but I could tell I was getting there. The taste of her kiss made me want to see if the Jameson still tasted the same. "Carol, have you thought of anything else since we talked this morning?"

She shook her head and stood up. "Nothing. I'm going over some of Don's notes and papers to see if they might help."

"That's good. How about the—" I was going to ask her if she could show me the few gems that her husband had appraised, but I didn't want to tip off Roxanne about that little secret, assuming she didn't already know. "I guess that's all I need for now."

Roxanne stood and walked toward me. "Sounds like business time is over, Jack. That means it's play time. This may be a good time for you to start drinking—the three of us—and see what happens."

I smiled at her. "Sorry, Roxie. I have plans. It's been good to see you. You look great, of course."

"Of course," she said, putting her arms around my neck again and kissing me—lightly this time, letting me feel the whole package again.

"I'll walk you out to your car, Jack." Carol turned toward the hallway as Roxanne patted me on the butt and made a "call me" sign with her hand. I nodded and followed Carol out of the room.

"Roxanne comes on a little strong, but she's been a good friend to me since Don died. She told me you two were … close." We walked slowly to my car.

"Yes, but that was a couple of years ago. To be honest, I don't want to get involved like that again."

"You mean involved at all, or just with Roxanne?" She was smiling as she said it.

"I mean I'd like to move a little more slowly."

"I understand," Carol said, holding out her hand again. I took it, and she stepped toward me. I had the impression that she was testing me to see if I'd make the inevitable move. God knows I wanted to. The moonlight reflected in her emerald eyes reminded me of the gems I'd wanted to ask her about.

"By the way," I said, still holding her hand, "have you come across any gems at all in Don's safe? You mentioned he had a few of them appraised some time before he passed away."

"No. I searched. They're not in his safe. I don't know where they are. Perhaps one of his old crew—"

"I'll check with them." I let go of her hand.

"Call me if you think I can help with anything," she said. "Any time."

"And you do the same. Good night."

I stopped at the guard gate, parked next to Don Masterson's security car, and knocked on his booth. He grinned and opened the door right away. "Glad you stopped by, Jack. These nights can get pretty bad."

"I bet. Say, Mrs. Chambers mentioned there had been some break-ins or other activity out here lately. I'm doing a little private work for her. Anything you think might help me out?"

Masterson shook his head. "Naw, Jack. People were stealing some of the King Arthur shit from the mailboxes and front doors. That's about it. There were a few reports about some Chinese-looking characters driving through, but that was a while back."

"Chinese? Are you sure?"

He shrugged. "Who the hell can tell those people apart?"

I laughed. "Well, you know what they say, Don. They probably think the same way about us."

As I drove back to my apartment, I thought through what I had learned so far. There were a lot of unanswered questions, and that was just the way I liked it. I was good at solving other people's problems, not so good at my own. I looked at my watch and knew it was going to be a long night. Too much stimulation from the luscious Carol and Roxanne. I wondered just how close the two of them really were. Roxanne often gave erroneous signals about her relationships. It was just part of her game. And she was a master player. I remembered every part of her in bed—how she felt and tasted and how she would cry out at just the right times. It may have been phony but it worked for me. *Right. No sleep tonight, my friend.* Then I felt my phone vibrate. "Probably set it off myself, thinking about Roxie," I said out loud. But it was only a reminder about my next dental appointment.

Roxanne had turned me on, but I didn't want to call her. Yet. Part of it was not wanting to get back into a situation that I knew wasn't good for me. Being with Roxie had started me on a downward spiral. I never got into drugs with her—the drinking was more than enough. And the women. Lots of women. There were no real relationships anymore. Just faces and bodies. I didn't want to admit that I had begun to enjoy it. I kept telling myself that if I had to have a problem, that wasn't a bad one. When you're a drunk, lying to yourself is easy.

It was still fairly early so I decided to stop by my favorite Irish pub, Mucky McCarthy's, in Alpharetta. Mucks was owned and operated by Erin Doyle, a shimmering brunette with a bawdy, black sense of humor I loved and a hearty Irish accent. We had dated, on and off, for a year or so. She was actually from Wexford, Ireland, and we had flown over to visit her family, an endless line of smiling, hard-drinking cousins. We both knew things were getting serious, but for some reason it never developed. Well, maybe the real reason was that the thought of sticking with one woman for any length of time made me paranoid. After a long talk, we'd decided to break it off and stay friends. Erin had been the last decent woman in my life.

She looked up as I walked through the door. "Well, hello, stranger," she said, smiling.

"Long time, no see. Or feel."

I sat opposite her at the bar. "How's my favorite brunette?"

"I don't know. I haven't seen her lately." We both laughed. "How about a Guinness?"

"A ginger ale would be good."

"This is an improvement, Jack. How long?"

"Nineteen months and some." I didn't say I felt like I'd quit yesterday and would never make it through the night. I looked around the place. "Not much action tonight."

Erin brought the drink to me. "And are you looking for action? What's the matter—Roxanne out of town?"

I took a slow sip. "That was a long time ago. I'm missing the good green warmth of the old country."

She smiled. "For you, that would be Norway, Jack."

"You know too much about me." I took another sip. "Look, I know this is spur of the moment, but how about getting together?"

Erin stared at me for a moment. "That's probably not a good idea."

"It's a hell of a good idea. I need a friend."

"Everybody needs a friend. Why me?"

I grinned. "Because you talk funny."

Erin did that shy-smile thing she always did, walked over to a phone behind the bar, and pressed a button. A guy I didn't know came out from the back. "Sean, can you take over for me? I have to visit a sick friend." Sean smiled at her. "Close up at the usual time."

"I'll do that, boss lady. Enjoy."

There was nothing complicated about our relationship. I liked Erin exactly the way she was and she reciprocated. She even put up with my Bobby Darin addiction. She wasn't hooked on anything but honesty, and that was rare with women in Roswell, at least the ones I knew. She worked hard and enjoyed her time off. In addition to our trip to Ireland, we had flown up to New York and Chicago and had spent a full week in San Francisco. Erin wanted to get married and have a family. As much as I liked her, I couldn't get my mind around that. She was great in bed and would curse in Gaelic when she was excited. Whenever I asked her what she was saying, she would blush and shake her head.

We made love that night as if we had never been apart. I didn't hear any Gaelic, but it didn't matter. She looked as if she would cry as we lay next to each other but that never happened. Finally, she got up, pulled on her clothes and shoes, bent down, and kissed me.

"Good-bye, Jack. It was lovely. It was always lovely. But no more." And she was gone.

I could have called her back, but I didn't. Why I didn't was another question I couldn't—or wouldn't—answer. It was a question I had asked myself many times. Truth is something alcoholics avoid. Erin was everything good and sweet and clean—everything I needed. I laughed a lot around her. I didn't even drink as much. I had always avoided coming to conclusions about Erin, and I fell asleep ignoring some obvious answers.

I woke up still feeling badly about letting Erin leave the night before. She deserved a lot better from me. I don't know why that feeling made me think of Tom Crowley—Father Tom, the parish priest at Saint Barnabas in Roswell. We had known each other since I was a rookie on the force and I'd called him for help with a domestic family argument. He was able to calm the people down. Later he and I went out for drinks, after we'd both changed our outfits. We still got together when either of us felt like it. We were about the same age and had the same sense of humor. Tom knew I was an ex-Catholic and that I had even spent time in a seminary in my younger days. But we seldom talked religion. Mostly sports. I called him and invited him to an early lunch at a little Asian place I knew he liked. Guess I had Asian on my mind. I was at a table in the back when he walked in, and I motioned him over.

"How are you, Jack? Good to see you."

"Pretty good, Father Tom. And you?"

"I'm good. And you can call me Tom, you know."

"Too much old Catholic in me, Father. I'd be afraid I'd go straight to hell."

He laughed at that. "So how is my favorite ex-altar boy?" The waitress came and he ordered some iced tea. I did the same.

"My Latin is still pretty good, Father."

"I wish mine was as good. We still do that Latin service every Friday at seven, Jack. I could use a good altar boy."

I took a sip of the tea, hoping it might be something stronger. "I may show up one of these days, Father."

He nodded. "You're always welcome. Any interesting cases lately?"

I had shared some stories of past cases with Father Crowley. Not surprisingly, they weren't too dissimilar from some things he had experienced. He would never reveal anything he heard in confession, of course, but he could talk very generally about things.

"I'm on an interesting one now, Father. Can't tell you much about it yet. I'll save it for next time."

"And how's your love life, Jack?" he said, smiling.

"Yours would probably be more interesting, Father." We both laughed at that.

"What about that, Father? I've always wondered."

"My love life? Well, I wasn't always a priest. There was a girl. In high school. My senior year. Jane. We got close. She was a nice girl." He sipped a little tea.

"Do you ever miss it? Being with a woman?"

He nodded. "Sometimes. The sharing. The kind of closeness you get only with another human being. They tell us to channel those needs where they belong—between God and yourself."

"Does it work?"

Another laugh. "Not yet, but I keep trying. Some of the young women in the Church nowadays, they think it's a challenge with a priest, you know? They try to see if we're interested."

"And are you? Interested?"

He smiled. "Not yet."

"Why not?"

He tried to look serious. "Well, I just can't stand their music." That time we both laughed.

We turned to sports then and spent about an hour dissecting every professional team in Atlanta. They all seemed to be having off years. When we finished, it was time to go.

"Let me pick this up, Jack," he said, reaching for the check.

I shook my head. "That would be another reason I would be sent directly to hell, Father."

We walked out together, and I went with him to his car. As we shook hands, I waited for him to say what he always said.

"So, Jack. Have you talked to your mother lately?"

"Father, you know my mother has been dead for ten years or so."

He held on to my hand. "I know. But have you talked to her lately?"

We stood there for a moment, looking at each other. "Not as much as I should have, Father."

"Don't ever forget your mother, Jack. I'll see you soon. God bless."

It had been almost three years since I'd been on the Kennesaw State University campus. Their history department had an instructor with a keen knowledge of the Civil War, my only hobby, and I'd taken several of his classes. As I drove into the visitor parking, I was surprised at how much the campus had grown. There was a brand-new parking garage, badly needed. Two new classroom buildings had also been constructed, including a two-story structure to house the English department. Relatively unknown outside of the Atlanta area, Kennesaw State had expanded into the second-largest university in the state system. The only things that looked the same were the kids. The liberal arts college contained the Asian Studies program. I walked up to Dr. Jack Neal's office a few minutes before two and knocked on the door.

"Come on in," he yelled out, and I entered a pleasant, well-furnished room. Books lined every available shelf and were piled on chairs, with several stacks in the corners.

"Dr. Neal, I'm Jack Novak."

Walking around his desk to greet me, Neal took my hand and shook it vigorously. "Good to meet you, Novak. Move those books. Sit down. Call me Jack. So you've been working with the police on the old Chambers murder?"

"Actually, I'm working privately for Mrs. Chambers. I'm a former Roswell police officer, and we cooperate with each other frequently, as we have on this case."

"Yeah. Hell of a case. Messy. More to it than any of us knew." His staccato manner of speech wasn't unpleasant.

"Jack, I know you were asked to look over the markings on the body. Can you give me any more background on what you found?"

"Glad to. Glad to. Had to hit the books on that one. Still have photos of Chambers's body around here somewhere." He reached into a cabinet and, without any shuffling, pulled out a wide pink folder. "Here it is. And people say I don't have a filing system."

Most of the photos were the same ones I had seen in Homes's office. Some were of different angles or extreme close-ups of certain symbols or patterns.

"See this one here?" he said, leaning toward me and pointing at some markings with a pencil. "Threw me for a loop at first. Had to call a friend at UCLA for help. He said it might be a mixture of Japanese and Cambodian, which didn't really make sense. Ancient. Unique." He was obviously pleased with the discovery.

"So what does it mean?"

"Mean? Why, it's a curse. It's a goddamned curse, that's what it is. And a whopper of a curse, at that. Seems like a little overkill, no pun intended, since they had already beheaded the poor bastard. Scary shit."

"What kind of a curse—I mean for what purpose?"

"Well, the man—this Chambers—he must have pissed somebody off badly. Interpreting the language was difficult. Maybe a revenge thing. Nearest I could come to it was that it damned him, his family, and his friends to a painful death and perpetual—what was that phrase?— *perpetual separation from joy.*" Neal took a deep breath. "They told me Chambers flew in Vietnam and had spent some time on the Thai/ Cambodian border. Lots of temples around there. Incredibly ancient stuff. That's the only thing the Khmer Rouge didn't destroy when they obliterated the country during and after Vietnam. Anything old was good. The rest of it …" He made a knife cut on his throat with his fingers.

I noticed that Neal hadn't mentioned any gems. "You think Chambers violated a temple or some other religious object, and some Cambodians killed him?"

"Pretty obvious. Pretty certain. Yes."

"Any chance that it was a good old American gang murder set up to look like something else?"

Neal shook his head. "Not with those markings. No, sir. You can't make this stuff up. That's the real thing."

I flipped through the photos a few more times. "Can you send me copies of these, Jack?"

"Sure. Absolutely. I'll scan and e-mail them as soon as you leave."

I gave him my e-mail address.

"One other thing. I don't know much about the Asian community in Atlanta, other than that we have a fairly good-size Chinese population. But what about the Cambodians?"

Neal shook his head. "Some, but not much. They keep quiet. Most live in the Tucker area. Keep to themselves. Had a rough time, you know."

"How so?"

"A few survived the Khmer Rouge atrocities and murders and came here to live. They don't socialize much outside of their own community. I know a few."

"Can you give me any names?"

"Can do. Wrote down two after you called yesterday." He handed me a piece of notebook paper. "Warning. They don't like talking. Especially to strangers."

I stood up. "You've been a big help, Jack. I can't thank you enough."

"Glad to. Glad to. Hope you come up with something. Finding out who killed the poor guy—good luck with that."

We shook hands, and I walked out of his office, through the Arts and Science building and out to my car.

After adding to my notes back in the office, I opened the envelope Carol had given me and took out the list of names and addresses, along with her check for five thousand dollars. The lady was generous as well as beautiful. Maybe she was generous with other things too. I thought about that generosity for a while and how benevolent both she and Roxanne might be with me. And each other. I knew I was going to try to explore that idea sometime in the future and made a mental note to bring it up with Roxanne soon.

I called two of Don Chambers's former crew members. Karl Cunyort was retired in Merced, California. Although it was only about ten in the morning out there, he sounded like he'd been drinking for hours. I let him drone on about what a great guy Don was and how much he was missed. He didn't appear to have any helpful information about the murder. Whether he knew anything, I couldn't get him to talk about the gems at all. It was a wasted ten minutes.

My second call was to Chambers's B-52 tail gunner, retired Chief Master Sergeant Tim Tomlin. Tomlin lived in Orlando and was working as a mechanic at Orlando International, the airport that used to be a B-52 base in the '70s. He sounded sharp and interested in what I was doing. When I asked him about the gems, he became very guarded.

"Frankly, Mr. Novak, I'd rather not talk about this on the phone. We'd be better off—and safer—doing this in person. Any chance you'll be down in Orlando sometime soon?"

"Sure, Sergeant Tomlin. I can fly down any time. Lots of flights from Atlanta. What day and time would be good for you?"

"I only work half shifts, every other day. This coming Thursday would be good. Pick a time."

"Good. I'll check the schedules and let you know. I'll probably get down there earlier than later if that's okay."

"That's fine. Look forward to meeting you."

My answering system had picked up a call from Roxanne, but I didn't play it back. I was still feeling guilty about the way I had left things with Erin. I should have asked her to stay the night, paid more attention. We could have talked, maybe worked things out. Just listening to Roxie's voice now would be a tease I didn't want to deal with. I ignored it and went online to check flights to Orlando, choosing one for the following Thursday, down and back the same day. Then I called Sergeant Tomlin to let him know.

I thought it was about time I talked to Don Chambers's kid, Hank. I remembered Carol's perhaps too-strong denial about any involvement between them, as well as Homes's suspicion that something was going on. Carol had included Hank's cell phone number on her list of names. I called it but guessed he was probably in class and left a message. I could drive up to the Georgia campus in Athens in about an hour whenever he was available.

Hank returned my call while I was eating lunch at Pastis, in what the locals called Old Roswell. Best onion soup in the Atlanta area. Carol had filled him in about hiring me, and he said he'd be glad to see me. When I suggested later that afternoon, he agreed and gave me his off-campus address.

Visiting the UGA campus was always a treat for me. Athens was a small southern town that had been blown all out of proportion by the thirty-five thousand students on campus. As with any modern university, there was a fair amount of tension between the local residents and the students, none of it helped by frequent drug and alcohol arrests, not exclusively on the part of the kids. I spent four of the best years of my life—well, five—going to school in Athens. I'd entered the army after graduation. Several of my favorite bars and restaurants were still in business. I called Hank and asked if he'd be willing to meet me at the Blind Pig, one of my best watering holes. He quickly agreed. I pulled into the parking lot at about four o'clock.

Hank told me he'd be sitting in a middle booth. The Pig was almost empty—it didn't get really rolling until later in the evening—and he was easy to spot.

"Hank, I'm Jack Novak," I said, reaching for his hand.

"Hi, Mr. Novak. It's good to meet you."

He was a big, good-looking kid, probably six-foot-two, two hundred pounds or so. Spiked hair, quick smile. I liked him right away. He ordered beer from the onsite brewery, and I reluctantly had a soft drink.

"How can I help you, Mr. Novak? Carol and I are anxious to find my father's killers. She spoke very highly of you." The kid was polite and articulate.

"Hank, I've spoken to the Roswell police and to a couple of your father's former crew members. I also spent some time with an Asian Studies professor at Kennesaw State." I didn't quite know how to broach the subject of the markings on his father's body, but he solved that problem for me.

"The police showed me some of my dad's photos, Mr. Novak, when Carol asked me to take a look at them. She wasn't quite up to it. They were pretty gross."

"I agree. Did the markings mean anything to you?"

"Not a thing, although Dad told me many stories about the time he spent in Vietnam and being stationed in Guam and Thailand."

I had been thinking during the drive up about the best way to ask Hank about the gems. Carol said he was aware of them, but I wondered how much.

"Hank, did your dad ever talk about any of his—let's call them adventures   when he was overseas?"

"Adventures? Dad was supposed to be a pretty adventurous guy when he was younger. Can you be more specific?"

The kid was smart. We were both feeling each other out. "I'm wondering if he ever discussed one particular incident that happened during his time in Thailand with you."

Hank took a long swallow of beer and lowered his voice. "You mean the gems, don't you?"

"Yes. Can you tell me anything about them?"

"I didn't know how much you knew or what Carol may have told you. Frankly, Dad was always so secretive about them, I wasn't really sure how much he had told her."

I considered that Hank was trying to distract me from his possible relationship with Carol. I had to believe that, if they had been intimate, the information about the gems would have been something they shared.

"Hank, it's pretty obvious to me that there's a direct tie between the gems and your father's murder. The police know nothing about the gems, and the Asian markings—Cambodian, I think—meant nothing to them other than leading to a suspicion about gangs and drugs. I asked your mo—Carol—if I could see the few gems your father kept in the safe at home, and she said she couldn't find them."

"Yes. That's because Dad gave them to me about a week before his murder."

That was a little surprising. "So you have them?"

"Yes. In a safe place, here in Athens. Please don't tell Carol. I wouldn't want her to be upset. Dad felt he was being watched and followed and didn't want to alarm her, but I think she knew."

"I'd like to see them. Maybe take a photo. Even better, if there's someone here at the university who could examine them and give us an opinion, it would be a major assist in the case."

He finished his beer. "I date an Asian girl. Japanese. Her major's the Far East. I haven't told her anything about this, but I'll ask if she knows anyone in the department who is familiar with gem stones from that area."

"That would be great. To keep things as discreet as possible, let's say I'm a friend of your dad's and that I bought the stones somewhere in Asia—Hong Kong, perhaps—and I'm just interested in their history. We don't even have to bring up the subject of value. I'll make up my story as we go along."

Hank agreed and called his girlfriend on his cell. I ordered him another beer while they talked. "She said she'll make some calls and then get back to us."

She called back in just a few minutes. We had an appointment with a

Dr. Chang for nine the next morning. Hank didn't tell me where he kept them, but he said he would meet me in the morning with the stones.

I decided to spend the night in Athens and called a few old friends. Two of them were married and reluctantly begged off. The third—a fraternity brother recovering from his third divorce—jumped at the chance. We spent way too much time hitting some of our old haunts. It wasn't as much fun when trying to stay sober. I went along as he staggered into the Boar's Head, the Arch, and Flanigans before he got really bad. I saw none of the old friends and familiar faces I wanted to find. I managed to break away around midnight, leaving my friend trying to seduce a coed about half his age. I had gone through that stage myself. Truth was, I was still in it. Maybe that was one of my problems—seduction just for the pure hell of it.

6.

I met Hank about eight the next morning in a local Starbucks. He gave me a pouch containing the stones, and we headed over to campus. His girlfriend Sue joined us just before nine at the Center for Asian Studies in the university's Camden Building. I had never taken any courses there but recognized the structure right away, close to the Russell Library. Sue was gorgeous, tiny, very bright, and eager to help. It was obvious she and Hank were in love, forcing me again to rethink the possible Hank/Carol connection. Not that being in love had ever stopped me from playing grabass whenever I had the opportunity.

"Mr. Novak, Hank tells me you and his father were friends and that you purchased some gem stones in Hong Kong and would like more information about them."

"That's right, Sue. I'm not looking for a monetary appraisal, although that information would be welcome. I'd really like to know anything about their origin and history."

"Dr. Chang specializes in Southeast Asian cultures and religions, especially those countries that border China, which is his real specialty. He has said in class that he's also a gem collector, so he is knowledgeable about gemstones as well. I hope he will be helpful."

Chang's office was on the third floor. We took the stairs. I spent some time examining the exquisite Asian artifacts on the walls and in display cases along the corridor. Chang's door was open, and we could see him sitting at his desk. Sue knocked and waved, and he stood to greet us.

"Sue, I see you found your friends." Dr. Chang had a fairly strong accent but he spoke very precisely. He was painfully thin and immaculately well-dressed. He shook hands with Hank and me as Sue made introductions. We all found chairs.

"Now, Mr. Novak, Sue told me you had purchased some gemstones in Hong Kong and that you were looking for any information, perhaps historical background, on them. Is that correct?"

"Yes, Dr. Chang. I haven't had the stones appraised, and I don't expect you to value them for me, but anything you can tell me about their origin or history will be very helpful." I handed him the pouch.

"I lived in Hong Kong for several years," he said as he walked over to a small metal table with a light attached, "and briefly apprenticed with a jeweler. I studied precious stones when I was younger. There are many reputable dealers in gemstones and some that are not so reputable. I am assuming you did not receive a written appraisal at the time of purchase?"

"That's correct, Doctor. I thought I was getting a real bargain and didn't ask for any verification of the stones' value." While I made up the story, I tried not to elaborate too much.

Chang grunted and sat down at the table, switching on a high-intensity light. He spilled the four stones in the pouch onto a velvet pad and picked each one up with rubber-tipped tweezers, holding them under the light. He said, "Ahhh," and reached into a drawer in the table, pulling out a thin volume with Asian characters on the cover.

"It is fortunate that I am an admirer of gems and know a little about their quality. Because the internal structure of all precious stones is not unlike our fingerprints, it may be possible to discover their general origin." He adjusted the light above the gems and moved them again, one by one, under the bright beam with the tweezers, studying them carefully.

"I have to go to class now, gentlemen," Sue said. "I hope you are successful. Thank you, Dr. Chang."

"You are most welcome, Sue. I will see you soon." Chang continued to manipulate the stones under the light, occasionally consulting the book beside him.

Hank said his good-byes to Sue, and we pulled chairs beside Chang while he worked. "I can now tell you with some confidence, Mr. Novak, that your stones are of a very high quality, although I cannot speculate on their worth."

"That's good to know, Doctor. At least now I'm confident that I wasn't cheated."

Chang stood up, moved around his desk, and pulled another book from the top shelf against the wall, standing on a small footstool to reach it. This book also had Asian characters on the cover. He sat back down at the lighted table, glancing first at the book and then back at a large sapphire under the light and then back at the book, occasionally turning a few pages.

"Most unusual," he said, almost under his breath. Then he said something I assumed was in Chinese, shook his head, and moved another stone under the light. Hank and I glanced at each other, not knowing what to expect.

"Mr. Novak, were you told anything about the origin of these stones when you made the purchase?"

"No, sir. I assumed they were from some region of China, but nothing was ever said." My cover story was getting more elaborate.

"No. I do not think so, Mr. Novak," Chang said, choosing yet another stone and moving it under the light. "These stones do not have internal characteristics and structure of any Chinese gems with which I am familiar, and they do not appear in my volumes." He smiled. "You might say the 'fingerprints' do not match. One moment."

Chang stood up once again, walked over to the bookcase, and chose yet another book. He consulted the index, turned to several pages, and uttered something else in Chinese. He then went back to the table.

"Mr. Novak, I could be mistaken. That is always a possibility, especially when trying to determine the origin of precious stones."

"I do understand, Doctor."

He turned off the light, placed the stones back in the pouch, and swiveled around in his chair toward the two of us. He looked grim.

"These stones have made me most curious, Mr. Novak. I can place them in Thailand or Cambodia. Their geologic signatures are quite specific. Yes, my educated guess would be Cambodia."

This was key corroboration. I now had evidence for Cambodian symbols on Chambers's body from Dr. Neal at Kennesaw, who knew nothing of the gems, and another Cambodian reference from Chang, who knew nothing of the symbols. At least this part of the case was starting to add up.

"But there is something else, Mr. Novak," Chang added. "I have studied extensively the religions, temples, and symbols of the countries of Southeast Asia. This is what you Americans would call my specialty. I would conjecture that these particular stones are associated with religious shrines or temples from a very specific area in Cambodia. The gems are quite old. We could carbon date them, of course, but there are only two places I know of where they might have been found." He paused.

"And where would that be, Doctor?"

"If I was a betting man, Mr. Novak—" he smiled at us—"and I am sure you've heard how fond the Chinese people are of wagering, I would say that these gemstones came from an area in the vicinity of the Cambodian city of Pailin, close to the Thai border. I know Pailin quite well, having spent some time in and around the town studying the Buddhist temple of Yiev Yat, a most sacred location to the Cambodian people of the area. I will say that I am one of few historians who have been fortunate enough to be permitted to examine this shrine and the precious stones associated with it. I have even published a book on the subject." He bowed slightly.

Hank and I exchanged glances again.

"There are gem mines near Pailin," he said. "But these stones were not mined very recently. In fact, they were not mined in any traditional modern sense. The edges of these stones have been slightly scratched, indicating they were removed from some receptacle. I am certain their age exceeds several hundred years. That is as close as I can come without an electron microscope."

I had no idea what to say. "Doctor, can you speculate any further about them?"

Chang frowned and handed me the pouch. "Scientists can speculate, Mr. Novak, but we prefer clear facts and evidence." He picked up one of the volumes he had been consulting. "This book describes the various temples and shrines of Cambodia and recounts in great detail the temple of Yiev Yat. Yiev Yat has been desecrated and almost destroyed several times over the centuries. Chinese invaders were perhaps first. Then various Mongol leaders. The British left their mark, as did the Japanese in World War II. More recent conflict and damage occurred during the

Vietnam War, when Americans became involved, not to their credit. When the Cambodian government was in a state of flux, and after the communists took over, many Buddhist monks, guardians of the shrine, were murdered. Perhaps butchered is a better word. The temple and shrine were largely untouched, but some stones were removed during each of those periods. It is known that, each time, the remaining monks, their successors, and agents stopped at nothing to recover the gems and exact punishment on those who took the stones and disturbed the shrine. Their recovery methods were—shall we say—indelicate. Beheading was their chosen method of retribution."

Hank and I were speechless.

"Because of the size and quality of these stones, Mr. Novak, I would suggest—speculate—that they may well have been removed from Yiev Yat." He picked up the last book he had been using. "This is my personal work about Yiev Yat. It contains spectrographic photographs of some of the stones I examined at the temple, photographs of their internal structure. They are virtually identical to your stones." He paused for a moment. "The last known desecration of the temple was by the Americans at the end of the Vietnam War."

"I see. Of course, I know nothing about that."

Chang nodded. "Of course." He folded his hands together. "I must tell you that if these stones were removed—" he struggled for the right word—"forcefully, the responsible party is in grave jeopardy."

"And why is that, Doctor?"

Chang looked very serious. "Asian cultures are quite complicated and enigmatic, Mr. Novak. I think the West refers to them as inscrutable. Difficult to understand. This is all true—even in our modern times. The monks of Yiev Yat are both dedicated and vicious. Their Buddhist sect, the Ikko-Ikki, unlike their peaceful brethren, is composed of religious fanatics who are trained killers. They have sworn to avenge those who have given their lives in the past to protect the temple. They will do anything to regain these sacred symbols, in this case the gemstones, and would, quite honestly, go to great extremes to recover them, no matter how long it may take. There are legends of these monks and their descendants continuing to track down transgressors and their families for many years, in many countries."

I was so stunned I couldn't think of anything to say. "I see. You said Buddhists who are killers? But I thought all Buddhists were peaceful, Doctor."

"Not all, Mr. Novak. These monks have dedicated their lives, and I might say even their souls, to the Devadatta Buddha. Many Westerners have never heard of the Devadatta. He was the divine Buddha's evil cousin and tempted him to leave the righteous path, much as the devil in Christian faith tempted Christ. As sometimes occurs in most religions, a separate cult formed around the Devadatta, dedicated to many forms of evil, including human sacrifice. Even the name of this fanatical sect, the Ikko-Ikki, loosely translated means 'single-minded.' They are a frightening group, with total devotion to their cause. They can be traced back to the 1400s. Although their origin is Japanese, smaller groups settled throughout Asia, ruthless guardians of shrines and artifacts of the Devadatta Buddha."

He paused and took a deep breath. "I do not want to alarm you, Mr. Novak, and I accept your word that you came into the possession of these stones quite innocently. However, my feeling is that in possessing them you are in considerable danger. Considerable."

"What would you suggest, Doctor?"

"First, I would recommend a further verification of the stones. I can give you some names of experts if you are interested. Then, it would of course be possible to contact the US or Cambodian government and have the stones returned. Above all, I would keep silent about your possession of these stones. Attempting to place them for sale on the market, for instance, would bring immediate interest from many parties, including those I have described. We live in an era of instant communication, and nothing remains confidential for very long, even to an isolated Buddhist sect in Cambodia. I must also tell you that returning the stones will not guarantee your safety from the Ikko-Ikki. They have long memories. Forgiveness is not part of their belief system."

It was obvious he was finished. "Doctor, I can't thank you enough. This is much more information than I expected, and I'm very grateful. You've given me a lot to think about. I may call on you again soon."

We shook hands with Dr. Chang and walked slowly out of the Asian Studies building. Hank and I sat down on some benches adjoining the library. "Are you as surprised by all of this as I am, Hank?"

"Surprised and more than a little worried."

"Do you think your dad was aware of what was going on with this Buddhist sect and the gems?"

"I think he was toward the end. I do know that he was very upset and concerned in the weeks before he was murdered. I've already told you he thought he was being followed. Then he gave me the gems and told me to take care of them."

"Have you ever had the feeling you were being followed yourself?" I said.

"On a college campus? I see Asian students all the time, especially since I've been dating Sue."

I handed the sack back to him. "Did your dad ever mention how many of these stones he had?"

"Yes. He said there were a lot of them and that he had hidden them."

"Any clue as to where?" I felt a little guilty about not having told Hank that Carol had promised me a commission if I found them.

"He said to examine his papers. That was the only explanation he gave me."

"And Carol says she has no idea, either?" He nodded in agreement. "Hank, have you got a good, safe place for these stones?" I liked the kid and was concerned about his safety.

"I thought so, until now. I don't mind telling you that I'm scared. Any suggestions?"

I wondered again about being completely truthful with him about my arrangement with Carol, but I decided to dance around the edges.

"You know that I'm working for Carol and am contractually obligated to her. I consider you a part of that contract. I have a strong, digitally locked safe in my office. No one but me has the combination. If you feel comfortable with it, I could lock up the stones for you. As further protection, I would leave the combination with your family attorney without revealing anything about the stones. My instructions would be to release the combination to you and Carol if—if anything happened to me."

"That sounds good, Mr. Novak. I trust you, and I'll be glad to get rid of these things." He handed me the pouch. "Carol can give you the name of our attorney. And I'd like your help in locating the rest of the stones when you have a chance. If what Dr. Chang said is true, I don't mind at all returning them to the temple in Cambodia. After all, money is not really a problem for us."

That certainly wasn't the attitude I'd picked up from Carol. She was definitely interested in getting the gems back.

"Be glad to help, Hank. And I think you'd better start calling me Jack. I'll be driving right back to Roswell. I'll lock these up first thing," I said, patting the pocket with the pouch. "Tomorrow I've got to fly down to Orlando. I'll try to call you when I get back. If not tomorrow night, it will be first thing Friday."

"That's fine, Jack. I was planning on coming home for the weekend anyway. Maybe that would be a good time."

"Great. I'll be in touch soon."

9

I couldn't get Chang's long, careful explanation about the gems out of my mind on the way back to Roswell. While I'd had a few close calls in my business, I'd always been able to take care of myself. Both as a cop and as an investigator, my army MP training had come in handy. But dealing with fanatical Buddhist killers, if that's what we were up against, was an entirely different story. Still, two things kept me tied to this case: a beautiful woman and the possibility of millions of dollars in gems.

When I got back to my office, I locked the door and headed straight for the safe. It was the latest design, supposedly burglar-, fire-, and waterproof. I wondered if it was Buddhist monk-proof, as well. The manufacturer claimed and guaranteed that its digital lock could not be broken. I hoped it wasn't going to be tested. As I placed the pouch with the gems in the rear of the safe, I took out my Glock Gen4 in its holster and strapped it on. I wasn't going to take a chance on what might happen in this case. Just the feel of it gave me some confidence. I also kept a bottle of very fine single malt scotch in the safe, kidding myself that locking it up might slow down my drinking. It seemed to be working so far. I ran my hand across the cold, smooth glass bottle but left it alone.

I checked my calls again and saw one from Homes, probably confirming our date to meet for drinks, and another from Roxanne. I listened to both. Homes was short and sweet. Roxanne was anything but sweet and described in detail what I was missing, using various parts of her anatomy to make her points. Since I have a great memory, she could have saved the description, but Roxanne was being Roxanne.

Just to make sure I got it all, I played her message twice. Then again. The woman knew how to get a guy interested. I figured it was about time.

She answered my call right away. "Hi, Jackie. Miss me?"

"Constantly. Look, I just finished listening to your call—"

"How many times?"

I laughed. "Three. I decided to see if you could really do that thing with the whipped cream and the bananas."

"And how about the chocolate sauce?"

"Yeah, that too. Are you busy?"

"Just peeling some bananas. How soon can you get here?"

"I'm on my way." Maybe Roxanne could make me forget my lingering regrets over how I had left things with Erin. At least she could get my mind off the monk murders.

My last call was to Carol to bring her up to date on my visit to the UGA campus with Hank. She said he had called her to check in, as well. Her voice didn't sound the same as it had—more nervous and concerned.

"Jack, I've made a couple of piles of the notes I found in Don's safe, but they still make no sense to me. They may mean something to you. Can you come over tonight to take a look?"

I wanted to see a lot more than the notes and she knew it, but I felt an obligation to have Hank involved when I looked them over. Besides, so far, Carol was only a distant dream; Roxanne was a sure thing.

"I can't tonight, Carol. I've got some follow-up work to do, and I have an early flight to Orlando to see Tim Tomlin. Hank said he was coming home for the weekend. How about if we meet about ten Saturday morning and go over everything? Three minds are going to be better than one."

"If you think so, that will be fine." She sounded disappointed, but that was probably just wishful thinking on my part.

Roxanne lived in a part of Camelot that had been constructed at an earlier period and wasn't quite as gaudy as the newer areas. I still chuckled at the rich extravagance as I drove up to her home. I usually knew what to expect when I saw Roxanne—attractive chaos. Still, it had been a couple of years, and my mind was wondering. She answered the door in what I would call a see-through dressing gown, but Roxie would have worn it anywhere, including to church—if she ever went to church. If so, I'm sure it was not the kind of church a wayward Catholic like me would consider joining. I made a mental note to ask Father Tom about that the next time we got together. I knew he'd get a laugh out of it.

"Hi, Jackie. Come on in and see what you've been missing."

"Actually, I can see it right now," I said, glancing at the gown. I stepped inside, and she came at me like we were magnetized. I don't know how long we stood there kissing but when we stopped my mouth and tongue felt as if they'd been used like a Roto-Rooter. There was nothing subtle about Roxanne.

She took me by the hand and headed straight for her bedroom. "Roxie, don't you think we should take this kind of slow? It's been a while and I—"

"It's been too fucking long, Jackie. We can talk later. If you still want to."

Roxanne knew what I liked, and she gave me plenty of it. There were times when I couldn't tell where any part of her anatomy was, and after a while I didn't care. Having sex with her was like mortal combat sprinkled with scotch and hot pepper.

When we finally stopped, she slid off and collapsed beside me. "Jackie, you're a wonder."

"I just try to keep up—so to speak."

"And you do a damn fine job of it," she said. "Why didn't we get married?"

I laughed. "It wouldn't have lasted a week."

"But what a week that would have been." She rolled slightly toward me. "And I'm insulted that you never asked. I'd tell you to kiss my ass, but you'd enjoy that. Or have you had enough?"

"Of your ass? Never. And marriage is something that has happily eluded me."

She smirked, reached over, and played with me for a moment. "Oh, poor Jackie. What happened to my permanently hard buddy?"

"Hey. I'm two years older and you're a lot to handle. Give me some time."

She smiled and got out of the huge bed. "Want a drink?" Roxanne kept a fully stocked bar in her bedroom.

I knew I was getting closer to drinking again and could feel a first-class drunk coming. Maybe. "Think I'd like some ginger ale."

"What you would like, Jackie, my boy, is to do it until one of us yells uncle." She handed me a glass and got back into bed.

"No, Roxie. That's what *you* like. I like it a little easier."

She put her glass down and began to massage me again. "You're full of shit, Jack, and you know it. Here's what you like."

She was right. I did like it. I liked it a lot.

When it was over, I was on top. I raised myself up to let her breathe more easily.

"I think I'm retreating, slowly and sadly, but definitely retreating."

I didn't think I could handle any more of Roxanne, but I had been wrong about that many times before.

"I've missed you, Roxie. But your drugs and the booze were getting the best of me."

She wrinkled up her perfect nose. "Oh, shit. Here we go. It's serious-talk time. I hate this, Jack, so spare me the morbid moralizing." She sat up. I couldn't help being impressed by her incredible breasts. And that new plastic surgeon husband would make sure they stayed that way.

"You don't need the drugs, Roxie. You've got so much else going for you. You're smart; you're beautiful."

"And rich. Don't forget rich." She took a deep breath. "Jack, we've been through this before. The drugs are part of what makes the sex so great and you know it. They make every part of my body ultrasensitive, and you love that, don't you?"

"Yeah. I love it."

"Look, let's cut to the chase. You and I love to fuck. You don't interfere with my marriage, and I don't interfere with your life. It's a perfect arrangement. Great sex with no bullshit."

She was right. She was always right about the sex. I leaned toward her and kissed her mouth, then her breasts, then worked my way down her body. "That's what I want now, Jackie. Slowly. Very slowly."

10.

The hour-long flight to Orlando was uneventful. Other than a slight strain in my stomach muscles, I felt fine after the evening with Roxie. I had stuck to my ginger ale, even though hangovers had never been a real problem for me—a typical rationalization from an alcoholic, of course. I always felt invincible after a drinking bout, and lying to myself was par for the course.

I brought some of my notes along on the plane and reviewed everything I knew about the case, trying to find the key, if there was one. When I got back to Atlanta, I would call the Cambodians whose names Jack Neal had given me. I wondered about showing them the photos of the Cambodian writing on Don Chambers's body. It might be good for a reaction, and I would have my Glock with me in case the reaction turned into something more serious.

Tomlin had said he would meet me in the coffee shop just outside my gate. I figured he was the guy wearing a Vietnam vet cap and air force logo jacket.

"Sergeant Tomlin," I said, walking up to him. "I'm Jack Novak." Tomlin was in good shape, in his sixties, gray around the temples but clear-eyed and grim-faced. His hand shake was firm.

"Just call me Tim. I haven't been a sergeant for a few years now. Welcome to McCoy."

He used the name of the former B-52 base.

"I see they've still got that old D model outside the airport."

"Yeah. They call it Memorial Park. People forget how long this was a BUF base."

I smiled at him. "That Big Ugly Fucker still looks pretty sinister."

Tomlin tilted his cap back. "You sound military."

"Three years in the MPs. Fort Hood, Eighty-Ninth MP Brigade. I'm quite a fan of the BUFs."

We ordered coffee, and then he brought me up to date on what he'd been doing since he retired from the air force. His maintenance job at the airport kept him in touch with aircraft, which he loved. He seemed sharp and cautious.

"So how is Carol doing?" he asked.

"Fine. I think she's become more concerned over the whole situation since Don's death. That's understandable. She's been very helpful."

Tomlin took a sip of coffee. "I haven't seen her since the funeral. She and Don were a great couple—great for each other. He deserved the best, and I think he found it with her. But I have to say she seemed different at the funeral. That sounds stupid. I mean, her husband had been murdered, so of course she was different. But she seemed to be changing somehow." He couldn't find the words he wanted so he changed subjects. "Don's first marriage was a mess."

"Tell me about that," I said.

He shrugged. "Nothing much to tell. Donna was beautiful and an alcoholic. She screwed everyone on our base in Barksdale, Louisiana. It was simply an untenable situation for a guy fighting a war overseas. She caused a lot of trouble for him."

"Where is she now?"

"I lost track. Don never brought her up. Last I heard she was somewhere in Louisiana."

"Any possibility she knows anything about this situation—the stones, specifically?"

Tomlin thought a moment. "I can't say for sure. It seems to me we would have heard from her by now if she knew anything. She didn't come to the funeral. I know some people who could probably bring me up to date about her. I'll call them if you want."

"Thanks. That would cover another base for me. You're probably right about not having heard from her." I didn't know a better way to get to the point of my visit than to just ask him. "Tim, it would really help if you'd tell me about your time in Thailand and how you and the others came into possession of the stones."

His jaw tightened. "Let's get out of here and go down to maintenance where it's a little more private."

The walk down to the maintenance area was short. Tim showed his pass a couple of times, and we entered through a door marked PRIVATE and headed into the bowels of the airport. "The crew chief doesn't get here until this afternoon. He said we could use his office," Tim said, opening a door along a corridor with several other doors.

We sat down on opposite sides of a large desk covered with piles of what looked like reports and graphs and obvious maintenance information. "I know coming here must seem silly to you, Mr. Novak. Maybe overly cautious on my part. But since Don's death—his murder—I've just had a growing bad feeling about the situation."

"I can understand why, Tim. And I'm Jack. Please start at the beginning and take me through the whole thing."

He sighed, took off his ball cap, and scratched his head. "We have to have an understanding that this is all confidential. Can you agree to that?" He held out his hand and we shook.

"Toward the end of the war, maybe January or February of '75, we had more and more time on our hands at Utapao because missions were fewer. And you can only get laid so many times in Bangkok. We wanted to go home. Our crew had become close with some of the Thai natives in the area, and we were spending more and more time in their village. Our copilot, who would fuck anything, was banging the village chief's daughter. He told her he loved her and would bring her back to the States when he got his orders. That was all bullshit, of course, but we played along. Happens in every war. The chief was proud that his daughter was going to marry an American. He thought we were all very special. You want some coffee?"

"No, I've had enough."

Tomlin went outside the office to a coffee machine, dropped some money in a slot, waited until the paper cup was full, and then came back inside and sat down. "One night when we were sitting around a fire in the village drinking local Thai beer—we called it monkey piss—the chief told us about a gem mine and a Buddhist shrine on the Cambodian border, not far from the base. He said the gems were very valuable, but that it was dangerous to try and take them. He had some friends who were willing to guide us to the place if we were interested. Made it sound like it would be a kind of dowry for his daughter when she married our copilot. We never should have agreed to go, of course, but we were drunk and bored and the idea of getting rich—well, you know."

Tomlin shook his head. "We took a couple of days of leave—we all had plenty of time saved up—and met the chief late one evening at the village. There were four armed men with him who none of us knew. Seeing their AK-47s made a few of us wary, and I almost turned back. But Don was our boss, and crews stick together. He didn't need the money but he was hot for the adventure, and so were most of the others. That was a funny thing about Don. He was a daredevil except when he was flying. Inside that bird, he was steady as a rock.

"That night, there were about a dozen of us. We set out in two old station wagons and drove as far as possible. After that, we hiked. It was jungle part of the way, but not too bad. Then our guides, or whatever the hell they were, made motions for us to be quiet and move slowly. We had been sipping from bottles of Jack Daniels during the whole trip and were feeling no pain. The whole thing is like a bad dream.

"Then this huge shadow rose up out of the jungle. When we got closer, we could see the outline of an incredibly giant Buddha. The chief told us this was the main temple. It was pitch black except for some torches around the outside of the place. You couldn't see a hell of a lot, but the guys with us seemed to know where to go. When we got closer, we could make out an entrance in the Buddha's belly. The gunmen led the way inside the shrine. That's where we ran into our first problem. Two monks were praying in front of a large statue—a smaller version of the outside Buddha, I guess. Only this Buddha was unlike any other I'd seen in Bangkok or in photos. We could see a lot of gemstones imbedded in the statue. It had a gold headdress and long gold earrings that looked like swords. The eyes were covered with a bright red blindfold. The statue wasn't smiling—the first statue of Buddha I'd ever seen that wasn't. In fact, its mouth was turned down in a massive frown. The Buddha's hands each held a long, curved knife or blade. A huge golden snake was wound around the entire body. The snake's head was coiled next to the Buddha's head—as if they were actually part of each other—and its mouth was open like it was ready to strike. But the really creepy thing, Jack, the thing that gave us all the shivers, was—" Tomlin stopped and closed his eyes—"it looked like there was a pile of human heads beneath the statue, as if they were offerings. I've always told myself they couldn't have been real. But they were. Goddamndest thing I ever saw."

"The monks became aware of us. It was obvious we had violated their code, or whatever the hell you call it. They came at us with these long fucking knives." He stopped and rubbed his face with his hands. "The rest of this is pretty blurry. It's not fun bringing it up again, Jack. The armed native guys with us shot the two monks right away. Several other monks seemed to come out of nowhere. I figured we were all going to be killed. But they didn't have any guns, just those knives. They didn't have a chance."

"Must have been pretty bad," I said.

"Yeah. When it was over, ten of them were dead. None of us had been injured. Our copilot was whooping and hollering like he was at a football game. Stupid bastard. The guys with guns—maybe some of them were Cambodians, I don't know—they went over to the Buddha statue, jabbering all kinds of shit. None of us could understand it, of course. As threatening as that Buddha was, it was beautiful, too, in that flickering torch light, in a creepy way. Gold and crimson. That snake—" He took a deep breath.

"Two of the men began picking or chopping the stones out with some kind of tool while two others stood guard. Funny thing—all the while we could hear this chanting or praying in the background. It may have been underneath us or outside; we couldn't tell. But if there were more monks, we never saw them. Then we went deeper into the shrine and hit the jackpot." He finished the rest of his coffee, wadded up the cup, and threw it at a trash can.

"We all saw those movies when we were kids—you know, the kind where explorers stumble onto a cave full of gold or jewels or some shit. Indiana Jones stuff. Well, we came into a room at the rear of the shrine that was literally overflowing with the most beautiful gemstones any of us had ever seen, just lying on the dirt floor. We had been told there was a mine nearby and I assume that's where those things came from, but I have no idea. The stones were smaller than the ones they had pried out of the Buddha statue. We'd brought large sacks with us and filled them up like it was Christmas. And we were laughing, not thinking about the bodies of the dead monks. What a fucking mess.

"When we got back to the village that night, drinking all the way of course, we split up what we had found. The chief took a sack and the four guys with the guns took a share. The chief wanted Don to have more than the rest of us, especially the bigger stones from the Buddha. So in the dead of night we headed back to our base with this big sack of fucking jewels. We told Don to take care of them, and he hid them someplace in the jungle, off base."

Tomlin's eyes were wide and bright, obviously reliving the moment. "That's when the shit started to happen."

"You mean the air force investigation? Carol mentioned it when we spoke."

He shook his head. "No. That came later. The next night we went back into the village to celebrate with the chief. The people in the village were all gathered together, chanting or singing. Our copilot's girlfriend came up to us, crying. Her father, the chief, had been killed. Murdered. Decapitated. The next three nights, the bodies of the four armed men who had been our guides were found on the outskirts of the village in the same condition. They all had these symbols carved or painted on their headless bodies. I saw two of them. It was a pretty gory sight." He stopped again and shifted in his chair.

"At Don's funeral, Carol told me about the markings on his body, and they sounded about the same."

"Tim, did the air force investigations start after the bodies were found?"

"Yeah. But not before the chief's daughter got it too. Same thing. Headless body outside the village; marks all over it. She was just a kid, for God's sake, and wasn't even with us when we took the gems. A couple of weeks after that, some of the villagers went to the Thai base commander at Utapao with stories about us. We denied everything, of course. And the language differences were hard to overcome. The Thai commander went to our commander. They held an inquiry. But translations were half-assed, and we stuck to our stories that we didn't know what the hell they were talking about."

"So nothing ever came of it?"

"Not officially, no. But we were warned that the investigation was ongoing. We pulled out of the base in early April when our tours were up and flew home in our own aircraft. That's how we got the gems back into the States. By that time, guilt had set in heavily on all of us. Even though we hadn't killed anyone ourselves, we were part of the group that caused the murders. A couple of us wanted to give back the gems, but we had no idea how to go about it. Ah, shit. Truth is we were also thinking about the money."

"So we agreed to wait for things to cool off and to let Don handle the gems. We figured we'd wait a few years and then convert them to cash in some way. Most of us were lifers and wanted to retire from the air force, so we didn't want any trouble. We sure as hell didn't want the investigation popping up again when we tried to sell the stones. Don said he had friends in Hong Kong and Bangkok, and he could sell them on the black market when the time was right. If any of us needed money before then, he said we could go to him."

"Did any of you do that?"

"Yeah. A couple of the guys who were down on their luck. Don made sure they were okay."

I thought things over for a minute. "Tim, did you ever suspect any of the air force investigators? Have you seen any of them over the years?"

He shook his head. "No. I guess I never considered that angle. I always figured it was some of the Thais or the Cambodians."

"I've got to say it's still hard for me to believe that you kept this secret for thirty years and never tried to get rid of the gems."

He stood up and walked over to pick up a black briefcase on the floor beside some filing cabinets and then came back to the table. He popped open the latches on the case and pulled out a file with newspaper clippings. "Don did try—a couple of times. Every time he came close— well, take a look at these. Maybe it will make more sense."

The clippings were about two murders of retired air force veterans, one found in California, the other in Michigan, both near military bases. One clipping was fifteen years old, the other about ten years. The descriptions of the murder scenes were almost identical. Two decapitated bodies. No mention of any markings. There was also a clipping of the discovery of Don Chambers's body in Roswell two years ago. "These are your former crew members, aren't they?"

"Yeah. Yes. I went to Donnie's funeral. Donnie Parson. He was the crazy copilot. His wife, Lucy, told me about the markings on his body. Donnie never told her a thing about the gemstones, of course. He was such an asshole. I just couldn't tell her the story. That's when the rest of us knew some bad shit was happening."

"What about the other—?"

"Jason Cutler. He was our EWO—Electronics Warfare Officer. Same story. Same headless body and markings. They found him in the snow in northern Michigan where he had retired. They blamed it on crazy hunters. He wasn't married. No close relatives. Don put up most of the money to get him buried right. He and I saw the marks on the body. That was maybe ten years ago. One other guy died of natural causes. That leaves Karl Cunyart in California. And me."

"I talked to Cunyart early in the morning a couple of days before I called you. He sounded pretty smashed."

"Yeah, that would be Karl. He pretty much stayed that way. I don't think he even remembers much. So I figure it's him or me next. Maybe Carol. I've started carrying a gun."

I didn't tell him I had decided to do the same thing.

"The two times Don did try to sell them, we lost two of our guys. He was all set to try a third time, and they got him. Jack, you're the first living soul I've told this to other than a Catholic priest in confession a few years ago. I hadn't been in a church in almost forty years. It was Christmas Eve, and I broke down inside that little booth and told him everything. I think I blew his mind. He didn't say anything for the longest time. Then he told me I was forgiven and gave me a few prayers to say." Tomlin half smiled. "I didn't think that would quite even things out."

I nodded, thinking of my own relationship with Father Tom. "Tim, have you ever noticed anyone you felt might be following you or keeping track of you in any way?"

"Shit, man, I think I see murderous Asians everywhere. I called Don about that, and he said he was seeing them too. Maybe we were both paranoid. He said he was being careful. Not careful enough, I guess. I decided I had a choice: hide and be afraid for the rest of my life or do what I loved doing—working on airplanes—and let the chips fall. I know they're coming for me, and I'll be ready. Listen, I babysat a twenty-millimeter Vulcan cannon in the back of that B-52 for twenty years while we dodged missiles and MIGs and other shit. If these goddamn monks want to play games, I know how, and I'm no amateur. I thought about the police, but this whole fucking thing is so crazy and it's been so long. Who would believe me? And, really, what could they do?" He looked up at me and gave me the half-smile again. "Maybe they should make a movie, huh? Except with a happy ending. You know, Indiana Jones gets the girl." He tried to smile and couldn't pull it off.

It took me a while to think of anything else to ask him. I wanted a cigarette again. And a drink. "Tim, I appreciate your time and what you've told me. I'll keep it confidential, as I promised."

"I don't really know you, Jack. And I didn't want to talk about this shit. I did it for Don and the others. All I can tell you is to be careful. I know these fuckers are out there somewhere, and they aren't kidding around. Anyone who gets tangled up in this is fair game. That's what I think."

We stood, shook hands, and headed for the door. He had left me speechless. Tim stopped with his hand on the doorknob. "People like me blame a lot of bad things in their lives on Vietnam. I know why I'm fucked up. I did one crazy thing. I never blame anyone but myself."

I had a couple of hours to kill in the airport after I left Tomlin, and I headed for the nearest bar. I planned to get as drunk as I could before they called the flight. Instead, I sat at a booth in the rear of the bar and just watched faces. I figured I'd be looking hard at every Asian I saw until this thing was over. I wanted to feel the Glock under my arm, but I'd locked it up in the car before I went into the Atlanta terminal that morning.

Something was keeping me sober. Probably Tim's story. On the flight back, I went over and over what he had said: the heads under the statue, murdering the monks, the villagers who were killed in retribution. And then his crewmates. I thought about Vietnam too. Just what we needed, another reason to hate that worthless war.

When I landed, I still wanted to get drunk and forget things for a while. I hadn't let go in quite a while. Not since I'd been involved with Roxanne. And now I was back with her again. And I needed it, didn't I? Sure, I was getting a little old for binges. Or maybe the binges were the reason I felt like I was getting old. I called Homes on my cell and asked him to meet me at TJ's. I felt like it was going to be one of those nights, and I wanted to be with a friend.

For my money, TJ's in Alpharetta was the best sports bar in the area. Families felt as comfortable as the guys who were there to watch games on the screens hanging all over the place. It was also the spot where Banks and Shane, a local "beach band," frequently performed. Banks Burgess and Paul Shane had been playing all over Atlanta since the '70s and had toured worldwide since then. They'd even opened the Atlanta summer Olympics in 1996. They had a great sound, and the audience had a fun time. Homes and I were big fans and often attended their shows. They weren't performing that night, which was just as well. I was so down from my visit with Tim Tomlin I wasn't in the mood for entertainment or sports.

Homes and I gravitated to our usual places at the bar. I spent a moment or two thinking about whether or not to have a drink. I don't know what decided me against it, but I told Homes he could let it all out as much as he wanted; I'd stick to ginger ale. TJ's was relatively quiet, and it suited my mood perfectly. Homes sensed I was upset about something and kept the conversation light. We kicked around a few old cases we'd worked. He was a good drinking buddy, and we had helped each other this way before. He could tell I was totally involved in the Carol Chambers case and that something had me edgy and on guard. We argued a few times over inconsequential things. His sense of humor always won me over.

When someone played a Bobby Darin song on the jukebox, Homes threw up his hands and suggested we call it a night. I drove him the few blocks to his place and then headed for my own apartment, my mind still churning with Tomlin's story and wondering what I would do next. That's the way I tried to go to sleep.

12.

had been dreaming about giant Buddhas with piles of human heads spread all around them. While climbing over the heads, trying to get away, I slipped. There was no way out. The more I climbed, the more heads seemed to surround me. Then I felt it.

You never forget the feel of a knife pressed up against your body. During my MP training, we'd practiced hand-to-hand, close-quarter combat for weeks, sometimes using Pugil sticks but most often with bayonets or other types of knives. Part of the training involved pressing the blade and knife points on various areas of the body to get the results you wanted, quickly and quietly. And if that failed, you could simply plunge the knife into any vital area. I'd never had to use a knife in actual combat, but I never forgot how one felt.

The knife at my throat was cold and sharp. It wasn't a dream. The blade was thick and heavy, that much I could tell. When I moved slightly, its pressure increased—without breaking the skin—until I stopped. But it came close. Very close. The window blinds were drawn, and it was pitch black in my room. I had no idea what time it was and couldn't see a damn thing. I could smell sweat—it wasn't my own—and raw meat. I thought about making a move for my weapon, but since it was on the dresser far across the room there wasn't a chance I could move fast enough to get out from under the blade. But I wasn't about to wait for the fatal cut. I had to do something. I closed my eyes, tightened my fists, and braced myself.

And then it was gone. In an instant the knife just wasn't there anymore.

I switched my bedside light on, fingers trembling, and looked around the room. Nothing. I got up and walked over to the mirror over the dresser. The thin red line across my throat was no dream. Neither was the open window in my bathroom, just off the bedroom. I could see nothing outside. But I did see smudged footprints on the floor—actual prints of a bare foot, no shoes. I could still smell the sweat and the raw meat. Through it all, I had never heard a thing.

Why hadn't he—or they—killed me? It would have been so easy. It could have been done in my sleep. But he'd waited until I woke so I would realize what he was doing. He wanted me to know he had me and that he could take me out whenever he wanted—a good scare tactic. Hell, a great scare tactic. I stood there, shaking, scared shitless.

The phone rang.

"Jack, is that you?" Carol's voice sounded strange and scared.

"Yeah, it's me. Just trying to wake up." No need to tell her what had just happened.

"Wake up? You sound like you had a rough night."

"You could say that. It was a rough day in Orlando with Tim Tomlin." *And this day isn't starting out too well either.*

"I'd like to hear about it. I know we said we'd meet on Saturday when Hank is here, but I wondered if you could come out this afternoon and look over Don's notes first?"

"Sure, I can do that. What time is good for you?"

"Any time at all, Jack. Just call me and let me know you're on your way."

I tried to go back to sleep, but that was a joke. I could still feel the knife. I remembered driving Homes back to his place, still tempted to dump the whole story on him, but something held me back. Finally I decided to clean up. I made a very light breakfast and headed for the office.

I put on a pot of coffee and added notes about my talk with Tomlin to the other case notes I'd been developing. While I was typing, I reached up to touch the holster under my arm. I had locked the door to the office—something I seldom did. I read through the entire case scenario. Tim Tomlin was convinced a group of Buddhist monks—perhaps their agents—had been killing members of his crew over the past thirty years for stealing sacred gemstones and desecrating their temple. He felt strongly that he was next. As I rubbed my neck, I realized I'd come close that morning to beating him to it.

I scrolled back through my notes to the segment about speaking to Jack Neal at Kennesaw State. He had given me the names and addresses of two Cambodian refugees he knew in the Tucker community, a suburb of Atlanta. Their names were Bourey Prum and Nhean Preap. There were no phone numbers; I assumed he would have given them to me if he had them.

I checked the Atlanta directory and had no luck there either. I decided to drive over and try to see them, maybe show them the photos of Don Chambers's body. I was looking for final confirmation of the markings from someone who spoke the language. I wouldn't reveal the existence of the gems, but I wanted to get as much information from the two men as I could. I wondered if there was a Cambodian Buddhist temple in the Atlanta area. A quick check online proved there was. Maybe there was a connection there; maybe not.

Homes called as I was reading through the notes one more time. He asked if I was okay. I said I was and started to apologize for my mood the previous night, but I knew that wasn't necessary. I wanted to tell him about my visitor with the knife that morning, too, but for the time being decided not to. Not even his kidding me about Carol and Roxanne, whom he had met several times, could cheer me up.

"What is it, Jack, the hot Roxanne? The lovely Carol? Maybe Roxanne *and* Carol—together?"

"Yeah, Homes, you know me too well."

I halfheartedly joked about women trouble for a while before he said he had to get back to work. His voice was concerned. He had my back, as he always had when we were on the job together. I told him things were fine and that spending some time with him at TJ's pub was just what I needed. He said what I really needed was to get laid, and I agreed. We made a date to meet for drinks the next week. I finished my notes, drank the rest of the coffee, and headed out to get some lunch before meeting Carol.

After lunch, I killed some time on the Internet, reading all I could about Buddhist monks, specifically the radical sect called Ikko-Ikki. There was plenty to read, and none of it was pleasant. The word *militant* in the same sentence as *monk* still seemed like an oxymoron to me, but it fit this group to a T. A huge group of Buddhist fanatics in thirteenth-century Japan had trained as warriors, becoming so strong they'd toppled the government of their province. For a time, they were one of the dominant forces in feudal Japan. They had one singular belief—total, wholehearted devotion to the Devadatta Buddha. Just as Dr. Chang had explained, Devadatta was the Buddha's evil cousin, and Japanese cults, similar to devil worship in Western cultures, had formed around him. Any who opposed them or desecrated their shrines were brutally murdered. Beheading was their punishment of choice. The monks gradually spread throughout Southeast Asia over the centuries, and small but powerful enclaves still existed. I grimaced as I read the text on my monitor. No question they were still around, all right.

My computer beeped, signaling a new e-mail. It was from Billy Busbin in Houston and attached were a few photos, a copy of Carol's old rap sheet, and, most interesting, the video Billy had promised of Carol making love with a woman. Billy's note said, *Jack, you should have a drink while you watch this.* Sure, as if I needed any encouragement.

Carol had stimulated me enough already, but I have the same curiosity many men have about women with women. The video clip was about five minutes long, with sound, and showed Carol and another blonde in bed, going at it pretty heavily. Carol was sexy enough by herself, but her partner added even more to her mystique. The things they said to each other were interesting too. The film ended with the other woman on top and Carol screaming. I wondered if I could make her scream that way. When I'd seen the clip four times, I was ready for the drink Billy had mentioned. And I was more than ready for Carol. And Roxanne.

I called Carol and asked her how five o'clock sounded for our meeting. She told me that would be fine. She asked if I would like dinner, and I quickly agreed. As I drove out to Camelot, I hated to admit that my mind was more on crazed monks trying to behead me than on the lovely Carol, despite the movie I had just seen. And I wondered how much to tell her, especially about the morning. No sense getting her more upset than she was, but she needed to know what she was up against so she could take precautions, as was also true for Hank.

I half-expected—and admittedly wanted—to see Roxanne's Mercedes outside Carol's castle/home, but there were no other cars in sight. The idea of having both of them at once was something I couldn't get out of my mind, for obvious reasons. Once again, Carol met me at the door, concern clearly showing on her face. She seemed distracted and gave me a brief hug before we walked inside.

"It's after five," she said as I watched her glide down the entrance way and head for the massive room with the bar. The lights were dimmer than they had been during my last visit. "How about a drink?

I really wanted one, but something made me hold off again. "Make mine a ginger ale for the time being." I smiled at her. "I'm still recovering from last night."

At the bar, she turned and returned the smile. "Anyone I know?"

"As a matter of fact, you do know him. Sergeant Homes Kenney of the Roswell Police."

She walked toward me with a drink in each hand. "Actually, I was thinking of a woman. But how is Sergeant Kenney?"

"Homes never changes. It was good to relax with him for a while. Yesterday was a rough day."

She took my hand and walked me over to the black leather sofa. We sat down together. "Tell me about it."

I swallowed almost all of my drink as I looked at her, remembering the movie. There was a good fire in the massive fireplace on the other side of the room, and I started to relax. "Look, a lot of what I learned from Tim Tomlin in Orlando is pretty tough to hear. I think you deserve to know it, but I don't want to scare you."

She squeezed my hand a little. "I'm a big girl, Jack. I had a rough time growing up, and then I lived through Don's murder. I don't scare easily."

I swallowed the rest of my drink and went into the whole story about the murders of the monks at the temple in Cambodia, the killing of the villagers that resulted, and the deaths of Don's crewmembers over the years. I finished with a description of the militant group of monks and watched her face. Just talking through the whole thing had given me the creeps.

"I didn't know about the murders of Don's other crewmembers. He just told me they had passed away. Of course, that all happened before we got together and married." She finished her drink. "Will you freshen these for us? Mine is Van Winkle with a little water." The woman was even first-class with her bourbon. I walked over to the bar.

"Carol, have you ever felt you were being followed?"

She shook her head. "No. And I have to say it's a little hard for me to believe Don would be involved with anything like you've described, but he did have an adventurous spirit or he never would have taken a chance on marrying me," she said while I fixed the drinks.

I walked back to the sofa. "I have to ask this. Have any Asians come into your life lately? Maybe some new people that have moved into Camelot? Anything at all that has made you suspicious?"

"No. I feel certain Don would have mentioned anything out of the ordinary he had noticed. Honestly, I haven't been checking for that kind of thing until lately."

"Unless he didn't want to scare you. I don't want to scare you either, Carol, but I've got to tell you this for your own protection. I woke up this morning to someone holding a knife at my throat."

She put her glass down sharply on the table. "Good God, Jack."

"He was playing with me, I guess. Softening me up. He could easily have cut my throat but probably didn't because he thought I knew where the gems were." I took another swallow of ginger ale, wishing it were something more powerful. "The son of a bitch was so quiet and my room was so dark that I never saw or heard him. I could smell him, though."

Carol put her hand on my arm. "Jack, I—"

"I can take care of myself, Carol. I was being stupid. I have a burglar alarm in my apartment that I never use. From now on I'll set it. You should be doing the same here."

She nodded and sighed. "Well, where do we go from here, Jack?"

I sipped a little before I spoke. "Normally, the smart play is to turn this over to some real professionals. I'm talking about people way above the level of the local police. The FBI or some other federal investigative agency. The problem is I don't really know what to tell them. If I start talking about stolen gems, bodies with no heads, and crazy monks ..."

"And we don't even have the gems yet," she said. "Jack, those gems are the most important thing to me right now. They mean more than anything. Because of Don. By the way, Hank told me about the stones Don gave him and the arrangement the two of you made to make sure they were safe. That's fine with me. Remind me to give you our attorney's name and address."

"Right. The rest of the gems may never turn up. Frankly, I think we should focus primarily on keeping everyone safe—you and Hank, I mean. Do you have a gun in the house?"

"Yes. In my bedroom. Don gave it to me for when I was alone when he was flying. He showed me how to use it."

"Good. We can talk to Hank about all this tomorrow."

She put her drink on the table in front of the sofa and turned her head toward me. "Jack, I've been through a lot of shit in my life. I can't even tell you about some of it. I'm a survivor. I thought Don was the answer to a lot of my problems, and he was. Then he was gone. For the past two years I could feel the pressure building inside, just like it did when I was single in Houston. I've been afraid I'd explode and get back into my old life. I need your strength, Jack." She put her arms around me, and we came together. I'd been thinking about that marvelous mouth of hers and what I'd seen it do in the movie, and I explored it until she pulled slightly away. "I want to tell you something. There hasn't been anyone since Don. I know what you may think because of Roxanne's comic innuendos, but not with her either. She's made it plain that she'd like to become involved, and she's a very attractive woman. But I haven't been ready. For anyone. Until now."

I reached for her, and we began where we left off. Her body was soft but more muscular than Roxanne's. She stretched out on the sofa and pulled me on top of her. I was so ready for her I was afraid I'd lose it. She sensed exactly what was going on, sat up slightly, and started unbuttoning her blouse. Her breasts were larger than they appeared to be in the film, and she had the most marvelous nipples, long and rose-petal red. I couldn't keep my hands off her when she helped me with my own clothes. Finally we were both naked. She stood up and took my hand, and we walked over to the thick Persian rug next to the fireplace. She lay down and raised her arms to me. I couldn't get the image of the other woman out of my mind, and I wanted to hear those screams. Instead, it was sighs and cries and heartbeats like thunder. Then silence.

13

Carol was scrambling some eggs in the kitchen while I sat talking and watching her. She had wrapped an apron—a tiny apron—around her naked body. Her firm breasts peeked out over the top. At first, I kidded her about how little it covered. Then I noticed her nipples hardening and asked if she was cold. She turned and said it wasn't the temperature, but I could warm her up later. She dropped the apron. We ate scrambled eggs and some kind of fruit drink she had prepared. She never put the apron back on.

Back on the sofa in the living room, we talked for a long time. She asked me to spend the night, but I didn't know when Hank would be arriving the next morning and didn't want to be walking around in my shorts when he did. She said she understood and asked me to come upstairs to check her gun for her. We walked into her bedroom. I was surprised to see it wasn't decorated in the flowery girly style I had expected. The room was huge, with a comfortable-looking reclining chair in one corner, a large television on a wall, and an elaborate makeup table. The king-size bed had no decorative pillows, and the bedcover seemed plain—even masculine. Probably leftovers from her husband.

Carol walked over to her bedside table, opened a drawer, took out a .32-caliber Beretta Tomcat, and handed it to me. I checked the chamber and saw all seven rounds. We called it a "bad girl" gun when I was on the force. Short and sweet. It was fine for ranges up to ten feet.

"Don said this was light enough and powerful enough to keep me safe. He taught me to shoot, and I became pretty good at it. It's small enough to carry in my purse. I even slip it into my sports bra when I run." She smiled and came toward me. "If I was wearing a bra, you could see there's plenty of room." I kissed her wonderful breasts and let my mouth and tongue roam all over that incredible body.

She pulled me toward her on the bed. She was still holding the gun. "Jack, you can hurt me if you want to."

"What?"

"You can hurt me. Pain doesn't bother me. I know some men like to be rough. It's okay."

I didn't know if she was kidding me or testing me, so I said nothing at all. I had the scream thing in the back of my mind as we made love again. She never let go of the gun, occasionally rubbing it on my neck and my back. For a while I thought that would make me too nervous to perform, but she expertly coaxed me along until I lost complete control. No screams from her that time either. She moved me around expertly to wherever she wanted me, and again I found myself remembering the movie. I wondered how many times she had played this "gun game" with someone else.

Later, she walked me to the door. We kissed briefly again and said goodnight. I don't remember a thing about driving back to my place. I relived every touch and taste of her while I wondered about the pain thing she had mentioned. And the gun. The movie images constantly replayed in my mind. Two gorgeous women together. Screaming. I was surprised to suddenly find myself outside my apartment. Back inside, I reset the alarm, fell on top of my bed, and was asleep instantly.

I woke up about three o'clock to go to the bathroom and felt the pull in my stomach and groin muscles. *Out of practice*, I thought, and I made a mental note to start getting in shape. I'd had quite a sexual workout over the past few days, after a long drought. I turned on the lights and made a quick check around the apartment. My alarm was still set, and everything seemed okay. I went back to sleep quickly. I dreamed about Carol and Roxanne making love while I covered them both in precious gems. That one didn't need any psychoanalysis to figure out. When the phone started ringing, my bedside clock read 8:30.

"Jack, it's Carol. Did I wake you up? I was worried about you."

"Just finishing up another dream," I said. "You were the star."

"I'm glad to hear it. Hank just called. He said he'll be here about ten. Is that too soon for you?"

"No, ten sounds good. I'll see you then."

As soon as I hung up, the phone rang again. Roxanne this time.

"Hi, Jackie. I didn't expect to find you at home."

"Why not? This is where I live."

She laughed. "I saw your car at Carol's last night. I almost stopped by. But I was too wasted to have done either of you any good. How was she?"

"Roxanne, you should know better than anyone that I never discuss my love life."

She laughed again. "I know you don't, Jackie. That's one of the many reasons I like you. The main reason is that you are perpetually horny. Like me."

"You have such a way with words, Roxie." I wanted to get off the phone, get in the shower, and have some breakfast before driving over to Carol's.

"If you've had enough of that skinny bitch for a while, how about a rematch? Bob's going out of town tomorrow night, and I'm getting restless."

"You stay permanently restless, kid. I've got some business in Tucker tomorrow. How about if I call you in the afternoon?"

"That's fine, Jackie. But don't forget. I've thought of some new things I know you'll enjoy." She described three of them in detail, one of which had to be anatomically impossible. Then she hung up.

I arrived at Carol's place about five minutes after ten and assumed the Dodge Charger in the driveway was Hank's. They both answered the door after my ring. Carol reset the alarm and we walked into the huge living room. Images from the previous night danced through my head, and I saw Carol smiling at me as we sat down.

"Jack, I brought Hank up to date on what you told me last night about your visit to Sergeant Tomlin in Orlando. I also told him about the man with the knife in your apartment. I've suggested he get a gun as well. He lives off campus, so that shouldn't be a problem."

"I think I'm getting paranoid too, Jack," Hank said. "Now I'm looking for Cambodians—or any Asian person—around every corner. It's even affecting my relationship with Sue."

"We're all that way, Hank. Maybe a good dose of paranoia would have helped your dad and his crew."

They both agreed. "I've got some coffee going in Don's old office. I've separated the notes from his safe and desk drawers into three piles," Carol said. "I also spent an hour or so on his computer, looking at his old documents and anything else that might give us a clue about the gems."

"Great. Let's get started."

Don Chambers's office was comfortable and well furnished, with leather furniture all around. Carol had pulled up small tables and placed piles of paper on each.

"Let's do this," I suggested. "We'll each take a pile and then switch until we've gone through all of the notes. Things that mean nothing to one of us may strike some kind of chord with another."

We poured ourselves coffee and got down to work. Carol had been through almost all the material, although she admitted she skipped over things that seemed to make no sense. She printed out anything from Don's old computer files she thought might help us out, and I ran a few searches myself for key words that might lead to something. No luck there at all.

Questions bounced back and forth among the three of us, and then we finally finished our note-checking and sat back in our chairs, right where we'd started almost two hours before—nowhere.

Hank broke the silence first. "Jack, I don't know about you, but I'm becoming more and more convinced that something has happened to the gems. Dad would never have left us in this situation, especially when he began to have suspicions about being followed."

"I agree, Jack," Carol said, "but I think—I know—the gems haven't been found. Don always assured me that the gems were safe and close by. If something had happened, he would have let me know. He said he wanted me to have those gems. I want them. *I need them*. You've got to find them." Her voice was loud and harsh.

"Unless the person or people that murdered him found the gems. Then all of this has been a waste of time." I was discouraged.

They agreed. "Maybe we're better off that way," Hank said. "From what we learned from Dr. Chang at Georgia and what Sergeant Tomlin told you, the damn things are cursed anyway. And so are we if we find them."

"Curses are nonsense," Carol said. "The gems are worth millions. Millions." She stood up and paced back and forth. "All my life I've been deprived of things I wanted. And needed. Things that were rightfully mine. And those gems don't belong to anyone else but me, dammit."

Hank and I stared at her. Then in silence we all thought things over. "We've got a few slips of paper from Don's notes with Asian, maybe Cambodian, writing on them that we still can't translate," I said. "I'm planning to drive over to Tucker this afternoon and interview a couple of Cambodian men Dr. Neal told me about. They may be able to help with this last lead. Any objections from either of you if I show them the symbols on your father's body to see if that will help?"

They shook their heads. "Why don't I make us some lunch before you go, Jack?"

"That would be great."

"Want any company on your visit?" Hank asked.

"I'd love some, but let's keep things as safe as possible. I'll go solo. I've got my weapon, and I'll leave the names and addresses of the two men I'll be seeing with you. If I don't show up or call in a few hours, call Homer Kenney at the Roswell PD and tell him where I am. I haven't given him any information about the gems or the Cambodians, but we may have to if there's trouble."

We ate some sandwiches in the kitchen in total silence. Not even the skimpy apron Carol wore the night before, hanging on a hook by the door, could snap me out of my funk.

"Oh, I almost forgot," Hank said. "I have something in my car." He stood up and left us for a minute. When he came back in, he carried a small booklet in his hand.

"Dad handed me this when he gave me the four gems. He said it was a kind of diary that reminded him of some fun times we had when I was a kid. He only wrote on a few pages. There are no hidden secrets that I can see. I read it at the time and forgot about it until this morning, when I read it again. It still means nothing to me." Hank handed me the book.

I opened it up and read through a few of Don's sentences. As Hank mentioned, they were reminiscences about some trips they took when Hank was younger—some nice father/son stuff, but nothing with any concealed meaning. The last sentence caught my eye.

Hank, of all the trips we took and the things we did, I enjoyed fishing with you up in Dahlonega at Dockery Lake the most. Remember what we used to do after fishing? Lunch at McDonald's, then fishing for gold. Then maybe some mining. When it was all over we'd head for home. It was always good to get home. Home is the most important thing. Remember?

"Hank, what does he mean about fishing for gold?"

Carol picked up the diary and flipped through the pages.

The young man smiled. "Well, we never caught any fish to speak of, and it became a joke between the two of us. We spent most of our time talking. We even camped out at Dockery once or twice. Afterwards, we'd get something to eat and then head for the local tourist traps in Dahlonega to pan for gold. Most people outside of Georgia don't know that Dahlonega, not California, was the site of the first big gold rush in the United States. It started back in the late 1820s. There's no gold there anymore, but they salt the old mines with some flakes and phony stuff, and kids have a great time panning for hours. I still have a small vial of gold flakes that I panned as a kid."

"Sounds like a good time, Hank."

"It was, and I still—" He stopped in midsentence. Carol and I watched him turn pale.

"Jesus Christ."

"What is it?" I said.

"The gems. There are also gem mines all over Dahlonega. They import some worthless stones and salt those mines too. If the kids get tired of panning for gold, they—"

"Sure. They dig for gems," I said.

Hank pounded the table. "That's got to be it. That's the clue Dad was talking about. His notes said *Maybe some mining?* That's it. We dug for gems. There was one gem mine in particular up there that we always went to. It had some funky name—Uncle Ezekiel's, or something like that."

"Wait. You think he hid his gems in an old mine in Dahlonega? Wouldn't that be taking a big chance? I mean, where would he hide them? Certainly not out in the open."

"That's just it," Hank said, his voice rising. "That mine closed down years ago. I remember the last day we went by there and saw the closing sign. I cried all the way home."

"Okay. So let's say you're right and the gems are hidden somewhere in the old mine. I've never seen the mine, but there's got to be a million places to hide something. What if the mine was converted to some other business? A lot of things could go wrong."

Carol joined in then. "Hank, I just read the few lines in the diary. I can't find anything that points to an exact location."

He shook his head. "I can't think of anything either. Jack, can you?"

I had reopened the diary and was reading it again. "Nope. There's nothing here. He may have—would you have any objection if we slit open the covers to see if he may have hidden another clue?"

"No, go right ahead."

Carol brought me a sharp knife with a very slim blade, and I carefully sliced through the front and back covers. Nothing. I was mad. "Goddammit. There are people out there who may be trying to kill us and we're playing hide and go seek with this shit." I threw the pieces of cardboard down on the table.

"You said you were headed to Tucker to interview those two Cambodian men," Carol said. "Why don't you go ahead? Hank and I will go over everything that we read through this morning—all of Don's notes. It's frustrating and time-consuming, but there's always a chance we may have missed something."

Taking a deep breath, I stood up. "Okay. Hank, check the Internet for gem mines in Dahlonega and see if any names sound familiar. Then we can all drive up tomorrow and look around."

"Sounds good, Jack. I'll get right on it," Hank said.

"I'll leave the prospecting to you boys tomorrow," Carol added. "But I can feed you before and after. I feel closer than ever to finding the gems."

"I'm headed for Tucker. I'll take the notes that look like Cambodian writing. I've got a couple of photographs in the car of the marks on Don's torso. If I feel comfortable with these men, I may ask them to take a look." I stood up. "Keep the door locked and the alarm on. Call me if you come up with anything. I'll do the same."

Tucker is a small community about twenty miles southeast of Roswell, one of the hundreds of suburbs that cluster around Atlanta. It used to be a kind of railroad town, but that faded as Atlanta grew and dominated the region. While most of the town had developed into typical little businesses, there were still a few farms on the outskirts. I guessed from my research that the Cambodians may have gotten into some agriculture. I could have taken I-285 and made the trip in twenty minutes, but instead I decided to drive down state road 140. It would take longer but I wanted to think over what we had gone through that morning, especially Hank's epiphany—if that's what it was—about the gem mine in Dahlonega. It sounded like a stretch to me. And even if Hank was right, where the hell would his father have hidden millions of dollars in gems inside an old gem mine? Why was that a smart thing? And how were we supposed to go about finding them?

As I got closer to Tucker, I took out my Metro Atlanta map, pulled over, and located the street I was looking for on the smaller Tucker city map. Bourey Prum's address was an old farm road on the outskirts of the little town. I drove up to a small, dilapidated house with a decrepit barn out back. The land didn't look like it had been worked for some time. The fence surrounding the place badly needed fixing. There was a dog sleeping in the yard but no sign of anyone else.

When I came through the gate and closed it, the dog opened one eye without moving his head. I walked up to the door of the house and knocked. After a moment, I heard movement inside and footsteps coming to the door. It opened slowly, and then a small, muscular, brown-skinned man eyed me suspiciously.

"Mr. Prum? Mr. Bourey Prum?" I had no idea how to pronounce the name but took my best shot.

He said nothing for a moment, studying me carefully. "You are police?"

I thought that was a strange reaction to my question. "No. Not police. My name is Jack Novak. I'm a—" I thought better about telling him I was a private investigator. "I work with the police. May I talk to you for a moment?"

Prum grimaced and shook his head. "No like police. I obey all thing. I wish to leave alone." He slammed the door. I knocked again, but he never returned. It wasn't a great start to the afternoon.

Back in my car, I checked the address for Nhean Preap. It was less than a mile away. Maybe I would have better luck.

Preap's house and farm looked almost identical to the one I had just left, although I could tell he had worked the land more recently. The fence was in better repair, and so was the barn. There was no dog outside, but a man on his knees was working in his garden, wearing a straw hat that looked like an inverted funnel. His back was to me, and he made no sign that he had heard my car. I picked up my files and walked slowly up to him.

"Excuse me. Mr. Preap? Nhean Preap?"

The man glanced up at me with sharp black eyes. "What do you want?"

His English was better than Prum's but he looked every bit as suspicious of me as the other man.

I decided to try things a little differently. "Mr. Preap, my name is Jack Novak. I live in Roswell. I'm studying Cambodia and the Cambodian language. I wonder if I could ask you a few questions about your country?"

The man continued to study me and stood up slowly. "You are teacher?"

"Yes. You could say that. I want to find out more about Cambodia so I can tell other people." I figured a little white lie wouldn't hurt, and I didn't want to scare him.

"You come inside," he said, walking toward the front door. "I have picture and map. I show you."

The inside of his home was small but clean and comfortable. "You sit," he said, motioning to a cloth sofa. He walked into another room and returned with what looked like a photo album, a handful of maps, and a kettle of what turned out to be very strong tea. He sat down next to me.

For the next half hour, I listened to him explain about Cambodia, in sing-song broken English while he pointed to places on the map. I paid very little attention to him, asking generic questions from time to time. As he gestured toward the map, I tried to locate the town of Pailin that Dr. Chang had mentioned, where there was a large gem mine with a Buddhist shrine close by. I had no luck finding it. Finally, when Preap seemed to be slowing down a bit, I interrupted him.

"Mr. Preap, could you show me the town of Pailin on the map?"

He glanced up at me for a moment. "How you know Pailin? You go there?"

"No. I've never visited Cambodia. But I have a friend who was in Pailin. He told me he bought some very beautiful stones there." *Might as well get to the point.*

Preap studied my face again and nodded slowly. "Yes. Many stone in Pailin. People dig for stone. My—" he struggled for the right word— "my cousin work there. He dig many stone."

He tapped the map lightly. "Pailin not on map but is here." He pointed to an area along the border of Cambodia and Thailand. "Very beautiful here."

"Yes, my friend said it was lovely there and that the people were very kind."

"Yes, good people in Pailin. Many people good. Many killed by Khmer Rouge after war. My cousin die. Not so many left." He looked sadly at the map.

"Mr. Preap, may I show you something?" I pulled out one of my files from Don Chambers's notes—the one that had the papers with Cambodian writing. "My friend gave me these notes from Cambodia and asked me to see if you could translate—to explain them." I handed him the two small pieces of paper.

He studied them for quite a long time and finally shook his head. "Cambodian not write this. I do not have the words to say what in

English. It is—" he pointed to the map. "It tells from here to here." His fingers bounced back and forth on the map. "I don't know. Sorry."

"Not at all, Mr. Preap. You've been very helpful, and I thank you for your time. You have a beautiful country. I hope to visit some day."

We stood up at the same time and shook hands. For the first time, Preap smiled. "You bring papers to temple. Monks have better English. They can tell." He grinned and shook my hand for a long time. "I give you address."

I sat in my car, looking at Don's notes. Great. How stupid was I, about to drive to the one place I should be avoiding—a Cambodian Buddhist temple—to talk to a monk? What if the note tipped him off that I was after the stolen gems? And what if he was from the same sect—the Ikko-Ikki—that was sworn to avenge the slaughtered monks and regain the gems? Maybe Hank was right; we should just forget about trying to find the damn things and leave everything the way it was. Carol would never agree to that. The problem with forgetting the gems was that I didn't think it would stop the murders. *So what the hell?*

The temple was about ten miles closer to Atlanta proper. The traffic wasn't bad on a Saturday afternoon. I could see what I assumed was the temple from about a block away. The building wasn't large, built completely of polished stone, with colorful statues outside. It was in stark contrast to the cheap, dull American buildings and businesses on either side. I had no idea of the days or times Cambodians held their religious services or whether I would find anyone at the temple, but I turned into a parking area. Just for the hell of it, I pulled out my Glock and made an unnecessary check of the ammunition. Comfort stuff. I took out my files again and included the photos this time. It was only a few steps from my car to what looked like a main entrance.

I rang a bell, which triggered Asian-sounding chimes, and waited. In a moment, the door was opened by a monk who bowed deeply and said in perfect English, "Welcome to the temple of Vihear. How can we help you?"

I found myself clumsily returning his bow. "Good afternoon. My name is Jack Novak. I am trying to find someone to translate some Cambodian writing for me. I have just visited Mr. Nhean Preap in Tucker, and he suggested I come to you."

The monk smiled. "I know Preap very well. He is a good, hard-working man. Come in, please."

I followed him into the temple and down a short hallway to an office door. The walls were covered with brilliantly colored portraits of older monks. We also passed several statues of Buddha, the friendly, smiling version, which gave me some comfort. The monk opened the office door and bowed me inside. He motioned me to a chair and then moved behind a desk and sat down. More statues and paintings of Buddha were prominently placed around the office.

"If I may, Mr. Novak, what is your business?"

"You could say I am a teacher, trying to find out more about Cambodia." *Might as well stick with the story that worked before.*

"At what level do you teach, Mr. Novak?"

"Ah, the fifth grade—in Roswell—at Barnwell School. And what is your name?"

The monk smiled. "Strictly speaking, I have no worldly name any longer. But you may call me Samrin." He studied me very carefully. "Teaching fifth grade must be quite a challenge, Mr. Novak."

"Yes. Yes, quite a challenge," I said, pulling some notes out of my folder. "Brother Samrin—is that proper?"

The monk smiled again and bowed slightly. "That will do."

"Brother Samrin, I have a friend in Roswell who spent some time in Cambodia. Close to the city of Pailin."

"Ah, yes," the monk said. "I know the city well. It was previously a mining center but is primarily a farm area now, as are many places in Cambodia that once had other industries." He paused. "We are still rebuilding after the horrors of war."

"Yes. It must have been a terrible time. But you look too young to have been involved in the war."

Another smile. "I may be far older than I appear, Mr. Novak," the monk said. "Now, what about your friend?"

"My friend gave me these notes." I handed them to the monk. "He brought them back from Cambodia but has been unable to translate them. I thought—"

He took the notes and laid the two pieces of paper down on his desk. "But this is not complicated, Mr. Novak. These are simply directions."

"Directions?" I felt my face turning red.

"Yes, these are a series of directions from the center or opening of a place that is not specified. That is all."

"Not specified? I don't—"

"The place is not named, Mr. Novak. The notes simply state—and I will write this down for you in English—the notes simply give the reader directions, the number of steps to take, from the center of a location—perhaps the main entrance or opening—to a final location. That is all." He smiled again and brought out a piece of paper and began writing.

Holy shit, I thought. Here's the big break in the case. My mind was flooded with dollar signs. "I see. Well, I appreciate your help. Of course, this means nothing to me. But perhaps it will mean something to my friend." I was trying hard not to look or sound excited.

The monk handed me the paper he had written on. "Yes, perhaps it will. It is most curious. A piece of a puzzle. Oh, and I can tell you that this was not written by a Cambodian. Probably by an American or an Englishman. It may have also been traced or copied."

"Yes, well, that's very helpful too, Brother Samrin. Thank you so much. Oh, there is one other thing." I had decided to show the monk the photos of the markings on Don Chambers's torso. The shots were extreme close-ups; I didn't think anyone could tell they were on a human body. I pulled the photos from my file and handed them to the monk.

"These markings may also be Cambodian. I'm curious about their translation."

The monk took the photos and placed them carefully on his desk. I saw his eyes widen, and he sucked in his breath suddenly. "Mr. Novak, may I ask where you got these pictures?"

"Ah, they are also my friend's. I assume he took them in Cambodia, but I really don't know."

The monk was visibly upset as he carefully examined the photos. "I cannot say the words—I cannot tell you the translation." He handed the photos back to me and wiped his hands on his robe.

"Excuse me, but why not? Are they not clear?"

The monk shook his head. "Oh, no, Mr. Novak. They are quite clear.

Quite specific. They are what you would refer to as a curse, a damning of some kind. That is as close as I can come in English. Frankly, this language is quite disturbing. This writing is, in a sense, religious. But it is also sacrilegious—at least it would be to anyone of my sect. It is not fitting or proper to be read aloud, Mr. Novak, or even in silence. Please, Mr. Novak, your friend—tell him he is in grave danger. He should seek protection. Now, I must ask you to leave."

The monk stood up quickly behind his desk and walked around toward the door. He opened it and extended his arm toward me. I followed him back down the corridor to the front entrance.

"I do not want to appear rude, Mr. Novak, but I do not wish to have that writing inside this temple. We are a peaceful sect. To have these words inside this holy building is blasphemy."

I suppose I shouldn't have been surprised or stunned, but I was. Maybe it was the tone of his voice and the way he carefully pronounced his words.

"Brother Samrin, I apologize for disturbing you and the sanctity of your temple. I assure you I had no idea of the content of those markings."

He opened the door. "I'm sure you did not, Mr. Novak. But you are the bearer of the words. And may I say that I hope you do not have a need to use the weapon under your arm. A most unusual possession for a fifth-grade teacher." He bowed again as I stepped out of the temple.

My cell phone began ringing as soon as I was back in the car. It was Carol; she was hysterical. "Jack, they got ... they killed ..."

"Carol, what is it? Is it Hank? I—"

She took a breath. "No. Not Hank. It's Tim Tomlin. They—He's—Jack, they found him. He's dead." She became unintelligible.

"Oh, no. How—who called you?"

She tried to regain some of her composure. "The Orlando police. There was a card in Tim's wallet with my name and a note to call me if—" She started sobbing again.

"Take it easy. I'm on my way back now. Carol, did they say—?"

"It's the same thing, Jack. They found his headless body inside his home. When he didn't report for work, they sent someone out."

"I'll be there in twenty minutes or less. Is Hank still there?"

"Yes, he's here."

"Good. The two of you stick close together. I'll be there soon."

I took I-285 thinking I could save some time, but that's a joke in Atlanta. Thirty minutes later, I pulled into Carol's driveway. I ran to the front door and rang the bell. They must have been close by because the door opened almost immediately, and both of them stood there. Hank was holding Carol's pistol at his side.

In the living room with the bar, I made drinks for them. We all sat huddled as closely together as possible. Carol had stopped crying but took a deep breath every once in a while.

"I liked Sergeant Tomlin," Hank said. "He gave me a B-52 model when he came up to see Dad one weekend, and we spent almost an entire Saturday putting it together. I still have it in my room upstairs."

"He seemed like a good man to me, and he helped me out a lot," I said. Carol was silent.

I didn't know how to get into describing my visit to the monk and what he was able to tell me. They were scared enough as it was—we all were—and I didn't want to make the mood even worse. Carol helped by asking me about my visit to Tucker.

"This may not be the right time to talk about it," I said, "but the visit went well and gave me a lot of answers. I can wait until later to tell you the whole story if you want."

Hank answered first. "You might as well let us have it all, Jack." Hank kept Carol's pistol in his lap, the safety on.

I explained about my visit to the Cambodian farmer, Preap, and then got into the part about the temple and Brother Samrin. "Samrin translated Don's Cambodian notes. They seem to be step-by-step instructions for how to find something, presumably the gems. They don't mention the specific starting point, but I assume that would be the old gem mine, if Hank's hunch is right. That, I guess, is the good news."

Carol's look was intense. "Then you know where the gems are?"

"Not quite. Let's say this is the first time we've had a real clue as to where and how to find them."

"Look, Jack. I say we go on offense. Let's you and I drive up to Dahlonega right now and see what we can find. We both have weapons. We can kick some ass if we have to. I'm tired of sitting around waiting for these so-called monks to kill us." Hank's voice was strained, but he was serious.

"Let's calm down and think about this," I said. "Did you find any Dahlonega gem mines that sounded familiar when you googled them?"

"No. But I know where the old mine was. I think I can find it once we get up there and drive around. Let's go."

I shook my head. "Hank, let's give it some time. There are too many unknowns, and it's too damned dangerous. Look, I may have been followed from Tucker. I was checking, but I was speeding and could easily have missed them. Or they may be on their way now. Let's be real; we've had enough warnings from these characters." I looked at my watch. "It's almost six o'clock. Let's have something to eat and try to relax for a while. I think we all need to get out of here—out of this house. We could all go to my apartment, but with just one bedroom I think we'd be more than a little cramped."

"I can stay with Roxanne," Carol said. "I have a key to her place. She has a gun."

"Good. Hank and I will head to my apartment. We'll stay in touch. Let's leave Dahlonega for tomorrow morning. I may even call Homes Kenney tonight and see if I can get him to go up there with us. Three men—and three guns—improve our safety odds. I'd have to tell him the rest of the story, about the gems and monks, but I think it's about time. We can talk about that later."

"Jack, I want you to use whomever and whatever you need to get those gems," Carol said.

After dinner, Hank and I got in my car and drove slowly to my apartment. It occurred to me that the people we were afraid of might very well be waiting for us at my place. Hank was nervous and kept sliding the safety on his gun back and forth.

"Better lighten up on that," I said. "Those things have a habit of going off when you don't want them to." I smiled at him, and he returned it.

"I'm a little concerned about Carol going over to Roxanne's," he said. "That woman's kind of wild."

I didn't think Hank knew about my relationship with Roxie and decided to make some conversation. "What do you mean?"

He sighed deeply. "I came home one weekend about a year and a half ago. Carol was out shopping and Roxanne was waiting for her at our place. She had been drinking and she—" Hank was searching for the right words. "She came on to me."

"Really?"

"She's a great-looking woman—don't get me wrong. A little old maybe. But I had started going out with Sue, and the whole thing just didn't feel right."

"Yeah, I know what you mean." Actually, it had always felt right with me and Roxanne, but I didn't want to say that to Hank. And I'd have to remember not to tell her that he thought she was "a little old."

"She started kissing me in the living room—the great room—and, well, I was kissing her back. She's hard to resist."

Tell me about it.

"Anyway, you know how she dresses. You can see through most of what she has on. We were getting into it pretty hard when we heard a car drive up. I thought it was Carol and said so. Roxanne said she didn't care. That killed it for me. The car drove off, and Carol came home a few minutes later."

I figured this was the scene Homes told me about when he thought he saw Hank and Carol through the window. "You sorry it didn't happen?"

"Not really," he said. "I guess she has a lot of men. It wouldn't have meant much to her." He could bet on that.

As we approached Roswell, I changed my mind about a couple of things. It was a little after nine and pitch dark. This might be just the right time to drive up to Dahlonega and check things out. There wasn't much nightlife in the little town. Hank might get lucky and find the old gem mine. In that case, we could try to locate the gems his dad had hidden, and if there were too many people around we could come back the following night. I also thought it would be smart to get hold of Homes and ask him to go with us. Not in any official capacity, but he would be an extra set of eyes and ears. And another weapon. I'd have to do some explaining, but I knew Homes would understand and back me.

I pulled into the parking lot of my office complex and gave him a call. He was at home watching television.

"Jack. Good to hear you. What's going on?"

"I need your help with a special project. Your discreet help."

"Okay, you've got my attention. Anything but holding up a bank."

"Nothing as easy as that, Homes. I'm in the car with Hank Chambers. We're about to head up to Dahlonega to do some—investigating."

"Dahlonega? Jesus, Jack, the only good-looking women up there are the kids from North Georgia college, and they're all down here for the weekend." He started chuckling.

"Wish it was that simple, buddy. Would it be okay if Hank and I stopped by in the next few minutes to tell you what we have in mind?"

"Sure. Come on over. I've got plenty of beer."

Homes's apartment was only a few blocks away, and the traffic in Roswell was fairly light for a change. He greeted us at the door.

"Good to see you again, Hank."

"Same here, Sergeant Kenney."

"Call me Homes. Have a seat. Who wants a beer?"

We both took seats on the sofa. "Homes, we're probably better off without any beer right now."

"Nothing for me, either, Sergeant," Hank added.

He looked at me strangely and seated himself across from us. College kids never turned down a beer. A ring-tailed cat jumped onto his lap, curled up, and started purring. "Sounds serious, Jack."

"I guess it is. And I should have told you more about this before, but the client confidentiality thing got in the way. The story is too long to tell you all of it right now. But if you'll agree to come with us, I can fill you in on the details in the car. The short version is that there's a good chance Hank and I are being followed by a few Cambodian goons who think we have some precious gems that belong to them. We don't, by the way. The stones may be hidden in Dahlonega, and that's why we're driving up there. These guys may also be the ones who killed Hank's dad, or perhaps are connected to them." I waited a moment to let him absorb that much.

"I assume you've at least considered going to the police with this, Jack?"

"I've thought about it, but it's a little involved for that. I'll tell you why later. Right now, I need your advice and, frankly, another gun in case we get in a jam. So this has got to be off the record."

In addition to being partners on the force, Homes and I had been good friends for years. He'd helped me out with a couple of scrapes with women and had never let me down. I'd done the same for him. Still, this was asking a lot. "Illegal activity" wouldn't begin to describe everything that had been going on. And after the knife incident, I firmly believed that the danger factor was very high.

"Jack, look. You're asking me to violate a lot of rules, any one of which could get me fired. I'd lose my pension, and, depending on how bad things get, maybe serve a little time." He looked down at the floor for a minute and then looked up and grinned. "So when do we leave?"

In the car, I told Homes everything, beginning with Carol's first appearance at my office right through my trip to Orlando to Tim Tomlin, as well as the guy with the knife in my apartment and my visit to Tucker that afternoon. Hank threw in some details too. Homes whistled once or twice but never interrupted. When I finished, he scratched his stomach and started laughing.

"I thought you only handled divorces and blackmails, partner."

"Yeah, so did I. And believe me, I wouldn't ask you to get involved in something like this if I didn't need you. I think I'm in way over my head."

"Well, I agree with that, my friend. And I see why you didn't want to bring the local police into it. This is an FBI deal for sure." He chuckled. "I knew it was serious when you didn't play any Bobby Darin."

We passed a mileage sign for Dahlonega: ten more miles.

"It's possible we can get through this tonight without any trouble," I said.

"Let's hope so. Maybe I shouldn't bring up the fact that you've had a car behind you since we left Roswell, maintaining the same steady distance. Might be nothing."

I checked my rearview and saw the lights. I'd been talking so much I'd ignored everything else.

"Jack, why don't you take the next exit before you get to the regular Dahlonega exit? It's the back way into town. Maybe we can lose these guys. If they don't follow us, it's probably a false alarm."

"Sounds good to me." I pulled off 400 onto a two-lane country road and turned left toward Dahlonega. Homes reached down toward his shoe and pulled a gun from an elastic band around his ankle. "Throwdown," he said, checking the chamber.

"Of course," I said, smiling at him. The car behind us didn't turn off. We all relaxed a little. We reached the outskirts of Dahlonega about ten thirty. The town looked like it was closed up tight, except for one bar with a large group of motorcycles outside.

"Drive slowly down the main street, Jack, and let me get my bearings," Hank said.

I did that. "There's the McDonald's," he said. "Now I know where I am. Turn left at the next street."

We drove another half mile or so. "Slow down here. No—go on." It must have been difficult enough for Hank after all this time, but finding some old building in total darkness was really pushing it.

"Wait. Stop here." Hank was excited. We were parked in front of what looked like an old Western saloon. It was not very big and falling apart—the windows that weren't boarded up had been broken long ago. "Let's get out and take a look."

"Hank, why don't you stay here with the car while Homes and I go inside and see if this is the right place?"

"The hell with that. I've come this far. I'm going to finish. Besides, how are you two going to know if this is really it?"

Homes had brought along flashlights and gave us each one. We made one more check for cars and lights before we got out. Nothing. Getting inside the broken-down mine, or whatever it was, was no problem at all. We pushed hard on what was left of the front door, and it gave way easily. There was dirt and trash all over the floors. The place had obviously been closed up for some time and broken into occasionally.

"Here. Here it is." Hank held up an old plank and waved his flashlight over it. "Ezekiel's Diamonds and Other Gems. Just like I remember." He was excited and so was I.

"What now?" Homes said.

"Well, I've got the instructions the monk gave me. Let's follow them and see what we can find. I'm assuming we begin at the front door. Let's see what happens."

For the moment, I forgot about the possibility of danger and felt like a little kid on a scavenger hunt. "Hank, you read off what the monk wrote down. Homes, keep looking out for lights and cars and people."

"Never stopped, Jack," he said.

The monk's instructions, copied from the Cambodian notes, were simple and straightforward. Hank read, "From the start—I guess that's the front door—take twenty steps forward."

"I wonder how far a step is," I said, pacing off what I thought was a normal distance.

"Turn right and take twenty-two steps," Hank continued.

I was avoiding trash and boards or kicking them out of the way as I walked. We were now toward the rear of the building, on the right side. Hank read several other back-and-forth directions, and I followed them as closely as possible.

"Turn left and take twenty-one steps. That's all it says."

I followed his instructions and then stopped. We were close to the very back of the building, up against a large pile of sand.

"Now what?" I said. "There's nothing obvious here. Surely Don wouldn't have just dug a hole in this sand pile and left the gems there. Besides, we forgot to bring a shovel."

"Maybe we can ask these guys for one," Homes whispered, switching off his flashlight.

Hank and I did the same. Outside we could see the shadows of two men quietly approaching the building. Homes and I drew our weapons and waited. The two men started talking to each other; it sounded like English to me.

"Hey in there," said one of them.

"Hello," I answered. "We're just looking the place over. Might want to put an ice cream store in here." I holstered my gun. Homes wasn't as optimistic and only lowered his arm, gun in hand, as did Hank.

The two men pushed through the boards over the entryway, as we had, and came inside.

"Ice cream, huh? I reckon that might go." One of the pair walked over to me and held out his hand. "I'm Thurlow Pointer. This here's my friend Justin." I shook hands with both of them and introduced Hank and Homes. We spoke in the dark.

"We're investors up from Atlanta. Had nothing else to do tonight and thought we'd take a look. Hope we're not disturbing anything."

"Heck, no. Ain't nuthin' to disturb," Thurlow said. "My uncle Dulcie owns the place. Ain't been nuthin' in it for years. You could talk to him, but he ain't awake."

"Wouldn't want to disturb him," I said. "We've seen enough for tonight. How about if we come back on Monday and look it over in daylight and then talk to your uncle?"

"That'd be good," Thurlow said. "I'll tell Uncle Dulcie. We live about a half mile down the road here in the trailer park. Look for the big gray double-wide. Number 23. If you boys want to look things over any more, why, you just go ahead."

We shook hands again, and Thurlow and his friend left the building.

"False alarm, gentlemen," I said to Hank and Homes.

"I guess," said Homes. "Think I'll just keep this baby handy." He kept his hand at his side, the pistol ready. "So what do we do now?"

"Well, we can't dig without a shovel, and I didn't see any obvious place to start anyway."

Hank walked over to the corner where I had stopped pacing off. "I agree. There's nothing here. I guess we could try to rip up some boards and take a look."

"Might as well, while we're here. I've got a lug wrench in my car. I'll get that. We can tear up a few floor boards, dig a little, and see what we find. The boards don't look like they'd be tough to pry up."

Half an hour later, we'd torn up about a five-foot section of the rear floor. I dug down as much as I could with the lug wrench—only a few inches. There was nothing obvious.

"I guess we should call it quits for tonight, guys. Sorry this was a bust. My hopes were high. We really need a shovel."

"Yeah, and if we come back with one, Thurlow and friends will show up again and want to know what we're doing," Homes said.

"Let's start back. Hank is spending the night with me, Homes. We'll drop you off, get some sleep, and figure out what to do next. Maybe one of us will get some bright ideas."

But no one had any ideas, good or bad. We made the drive back in sullen silence.

As we drove into Homes's parking area, he opened the door slightly and then turned back toward me. "Jack, I just want to say one thing about this whole evening. Thanks for not playing that goddamned Bobby Darin CD tonight."

We turned into my complex just before one in the morning. There were still lights on in several of the apartments, and I heard some music and laughter—a typical Saturday night. Hank had brought a small overnight bag with him.

"I'll be glad to get a little rest," he said. "I haven't been sleeping very well."

I pulled my weapon, opened the door to my apartment, and switched on the lights. We both stepped inside. I glanced at the alarm and realized I had not reset it before I left the apartment. I looked around quickly; nothing seemed out of place. *So far, so good*. I reholstered the Glock.

"You can have the pullout sofa or the bed, Hank. All the same to me."

"The sofa's fine, Jack." Hank walked over and set his bag down.

"I'll get some sheets. They may even be clean." I headed for the bedroom and heard Hank take off his shoes and drop them on the floor. He must have been tired. When I walked back into the living room, a man was standing over Hank's body. It wasn't shoes that had hit the floor; it was Hank. I was reaching for my gun when everything went black.

I heard a siren way off in the distance, slowly getting louder. It took me a minute or so to realize it wasn't a siren. It was Hank, screaming. I was stretched out on a cot, my hands tied behind me. Blood was running down the back of my head. It hurt like hell. I wanted to get up and help Hank, but my body just wouldn't cooperate. Slowly, I got to my feet and looked around. A light in the ceiling of a small room showed a dirt floor—I could recognize nothing. I made my way to a door and started kicking it and generally raising hell. It was all I could think to do.

The door burst open, and a small, familiar-looking brown man came into the room. He was stripped to the waist, well muscled, and wearing what looked like a red loincloth. His entire body was tattooed with an elaborate, blood red dragon. The dragon's head was directly under his chin; the creature's body stretched down the man's own body, the dragon's arms and legs tattooed along the man's arms and legs. If this was all meant to intimidate, it was working. After a moment, I could make out his face. It was Bourey Prum, the Cambodian farmer I had first met—the one who refused to talk to me. A knife was wedged into his belt, and his hands were covered with blood.

"Where's Hank?" I yelled at him.

He grabbed my shirt. "You come. You talk."

He dragged me into a larger, well-lighted room. In one corner was an imposing, grotesque Buddha matching the description Tim Tomlin had given me of the one he saw in the jungle. The Buddha's sneer seemed to be aimed directly at me. A large sword lay across the altar beneath the statue. I couldn't stop myself from glancing at the base of the Buddha to see if there were any human heads. I didn't want Hank's and mine to be the first.

Hank was suspended in midair from large wooden beams, his arms stretched behind him. Ropes were attached to his arms and ran to pulleys. As I came into the room, a man alternately tightened and then loosened them, pulling Hank's arms back so that he looked like a misshapen puppet. His scream was horrible.

"Stop that shit!" I yelled to the men.

"You talk. You tell."

"Tell what? I don't know anything."

Prum came toward me and pulled out his knife. "You know about sacred stone. Belong in temple. You have stone."

I wondered where our guns were and why he wasn't using them.

"What stone? I don't have any stone." Playing dumb was playing for time.

He slapped me hard, and the other man turned the pulleys. Mercifully, Hank had passed out.

"We know you have stone," Prum said. "We follow. You have. Sacred stone belong in temple." He gestured toward Hank. "He has. You tell."

Alone in this room we didn't have a chance. It was obvious they would kill us soon.

As if to underscore that feeling, Prum shouted, "You tell or boy die. Then you die."

"Okay, okay. I can show you where the stones are."

"No show. You tell now."

I shook my head. "The stones are hidden. Well hidden. Far away." I had no idea how much English he understood.

"You hide stone?"

"No. The boy's father. He hide stones. I know where. I show you."

The two men talked for a few minutes. They appeared to be arguing, but it was hard to tell. I had no idea what to do or say next, but I knew I had to get both of us out of there. Prum walked back to me.

"You tell now or you die. Boy die first." He waived his knife.

"Only the boy knows where the stones are," I said, trying to figure something out quickly. "I can take you there, but only he knows."

The two men talked again. "Why boy not talk?" Prum asked.

"I don't know. Maybe he wanted to see if I was alive."

Prum shook his head. "You take me to stone." He gestured to his friend. "He stay here with boy. If we not find stone, you both die."

I knew we would die anyway. "No. You'll never find the stones without both of us. I know where to go, but the boy knows where they are hidden." I hoped I didn't sound as desperate as I felt.

More arguing between the two followed. Finally they agreed on something. They lowered Hank to the ground. I saw his eyes slowly open. He looked terrible.

"You carry boy to car. We go in your car. Now."

I guessed then that one of them had driven my car from Roswell. Prum gestured with his knife toward what I thought was the front door before he cut through the ropes on my hands. I carefully helped Hank up. When his arms began to resume their normal position and the blood began to circulate again he screamed. His face was horribly bruised, his shirt torn and covered with blood, probably from the same kind of head wound I had. While Prum pulled on pants and a jacket, the other man cut the ropes from under Hank's shoulders. They had bitten deeply into his flesh, and as they pulled loose, he passed out again. *Just as well.*

"He needs help," I told them, "or he won't be able to tell us where the stones are."

"First we get stone, then boy get help."

Sure. I knew what kind of help that would be.

The two men spoke again, and Prum left the room for a moment, returning with another cot. The other man pulled some clothes on while Prum opened up the cot. Then they placed Hank on it. Then they gestured to me to pick up one end; Prum supported the other. As we all walked slowly outside, I saw that we were in the old barn on Prum's property. I knew there were no neighbors for miles. *Great place for a murder.* We walked toward the rear of the barn. I could make out my car in the darkness.

"You drive slow," Prum said. "No trick. I sit with boy in back. He—" he motioned to the other man—"he sit with you. No trick, or both die." His English was good enough for me to get that. I still had no idea what I was going to do, but I figured getting Hank loose and leaving the barn was a good start.

We stopped at my car and lowered Hank's cot to the ground. Prum opened the backdoor and motioned for me to lift my end. We slid him into the backseat, leaving a small space where Prum could sit. As I reached for the driver's door handle, a high-intensity light hit us and lit up the night.

"All right, all of you on the ground. Now!"

Homes was crouched behind the door of his truck, his pistol aimed at us. I hit the ground quickly. Prum yelled at the other man and dove under the car. The man screamed something, pulled his knife from his waist, and started running toward Homes. I was about to yell to Homes to watch it, but that wasn't necessary. I heard two shots and saw the muzzle flashes from his weapon. The man cried out, threw up his arms, and fell face-first to the ground. Homes always aimed to kill.

"Where's the other fucker?" Homes yelled at me.

"Under the car, I think," I said, not changing my position. "He has a knife, but I didn't see any gun."

Homes had a floodlight on the side of his truck and moved it over the area. I was able to see under my car, but I couldn't make out anything. "I can't see him."

"Me either," Homes said. "How's Hank?"

I rolled onto my side. "Not good. We need to get him to a hospital."

Homes walked slowly toward me, holding his pistol in combat position. "I saw a shadow moving into the woods—that must have been him. It sure as hell wasn't the dude I nailed."

"Fuck him for now," I said. "Let's see to Hank."

"Okay, here's the plan. Can Hank be moved as far as Roswell to North Fulton Hospital?"

"I don't know. He doesn't look good, but I don't think he's dying. Why all the way back to Roswell?"

Homes had his back to me, his gun held out in front. "Because, Jack, we're liable to have a lot of explaining to do. I can explain it better at North Fulton than I can down here, where I don't know anybody."

"Makes sense to me. Let's do it." Homes locked his truck and got into the backseat of my car with Hank. "My watch is gone. What time is it?" I said.

"About two thirty. Don't speed, but make some time if you can."

As we headed to the hospital, Homes brought me up to date. After we had dropped him off, he called my apartment and got no answer, so he figured some kind of shit had hit the fan. Then he called Carol's cell—"I still had the chick's number, just in case," he said—and explained things. They both figured we were in trouble, probably with the Cambodians. She gave Holmes the two addresses I had given her that afternoon, and Homes headed straight for Tucker. When he arrived at Pram's, he hid his truck in the shadows and went up to the barn. When he saw my car, he sneaked around and was able to hear a little of what was going on. Then he heard Hank screaming. He saw me come into the room, listened to the conversation, and then waited for us to come out.

"I owe you one, buddy," I said.

"You owe me about five, you bastard."

"Five it is."

Hank groaned a little. "Only a little longer," I said. "Hang on, Hank."

"How's your head?" Homes said. "Looks like the bleeding has stopped."

"Hurts like hell, but I guess it's nothing serious. I'm not groggy or sleepy."

As we drove up to the hospital, Homes said, "Park right in front of emergency. I've been here a million times on cop stuff. They all know me. I'll get him looked at and treated right away, no questions asked."

Homes was as good as his word. He went into the emergency entrance and came right back out with two men I guessed were either male nurses or doctors. They carefully slid Hank out of the backseat onto a stretcher and brought him inside.

As I started to get out, Homes shook his head at me. "You stay here, Jack. I want them to deal only with me. I'll give them Hank's name, your address, and my cell. As far as they know, this is police business. I'll tell them I'll be back soon to clean up the loose ends." He headed for the entrance again.

I was in no position to argue; Homes knew what he was doing. In a minute, he was back and got into the passenger seat. "Let's get moving, buddy. Our work isn't over."

"Moving where?"

"Back to Tucker and that bastard's farm. My truck is still there. So is a dead body. I need to do some cleaning up so I don't get caught in the middle of this shit."

"I think we're already in the middle of it, Homes." He grunted, and I headed for Tucker.

It was still dark when we got there. "No bright lights, Jack. Let's see what we can find." He handed me a flashlight.

We both got out of the car, Homes with gun in hand, and headed for the barn. We located the spot where my car had been parked. There was no body on the ground.

"Great. Now we have a disappearing body," Homes said. "Let's check inside the barn."

The body wasn't inside either. Under the flickering torchlight, Homes had his first up-close look at the Buddha and the arm-stretching device, as well as a good deal of blood on the floor. "Jesus, Jack, these are mean fuckers."

"Yeah. Terminally mean." We moved into the smaller room where I had been kept. Nothing there.

"Check this closet," Homes said. We found Hank's gun and mine, our wristwatches, and our wallets. "This is good. Saves a lot of explaining. With any luck, they'll never know you were here."

"Aren't you going to call the police?"

"Jack," Homes said, smiling, "I *am* the police." He found an old rag and wiped down any obvious areas Hank and I may have touched. "We need to be quick but careful. This place is pretty far out, but if someone has called the cops, we're screwed."

"Right. What about Prum?"

"Who?"

"The Cambodian guy who got away."

Homes shrugged and shook his head. "Let's get the fuck out of here."

"Right. We can use our cells to keep in touch on the drive back." We left for Roswell just as we could see faint traces of dawn.

Homes called me when we were about ten minutes away.

"My buddy, Dr. Dawson, just called from the hospital. He says Hank is weak but okay. No concussion. They gave him some blood, and he's going to have surgery on his left arm. It'll be in a cast for a while. The other arm will be sore as hell, but he'll heal and be fine."

"That's great news. Can you call Carol and pass it along?"

"Sure. And you're going to stay with me tonight," Homes said. "Sorry I don't have any women."

It was hard to smile, but I managed a small one. "This may be one of the few times I'm glad to hear that. I hurt like hell. I could sleep for a month."

We drove into Homes's apartment complex. He parked away from his usual spot. I was a few spaces farther from him. As we walked up to the building, he handed me one of the guns we'd rescued from the farm house. "Just in case," he said. Before entering his apartment, we both listened carefully at the door. Nothing. "You remember the drill, Jack. It'll be just like old times."

I nodded and leveled my weapon. Our team was back together. Homes opened the door slowly and flipped on the lights. There was none of that moving around in the dark shit you see on television. When he glanced at me, I followed him inside.

I covered him while he checked each of the rooms in the apartment, as well as the windows. Finally, he took a deep breath and sat down on the sofa. "I think we're okay. None of the windows have been jimmied or even scratched. Same for the front door. The place is clean. For now. I set my security alarm."

"Good. Let's get some sleep, if we can. I need to get my head straight." I stood up and turned toward him. "Homes, about tonight ..."

"Yeah, what about it?"

"When we were partnered, you said you had killed three men. So tonight—"

"Tonight was four, partner. And I know what you want to ask. I'm okay. It was him or us, and I'd already seen some of their work through the window of the barn. He came at me and I clipped him. No regrets."

I nodded. I had stayed over at Homes's place before and knew the layout, and I headed for the spare bedroom.

"You need anything?"

"No, I'll be fine. Homes, thanks for everything tonight. If you hadn't shown up—"

"Ah, go screw yourself," he said, smiling. "Truth is, I was ready to kill you myself if you started playing that Bobby Darin shit. Nighty night."

The smell of bacon woke me. It was two in the afternoon. I heard Homes banging around in the kitchen.

"I didn't know you could cook," I said, walking up to him.

"I can't. How's your head?"

I helped myself to a glass of water and sat in the kitchen bar area while he added some eggs to the bacon on the stove. "Just a dull throb now."

"The hospital called. Hank is improving. They operated on his arm this morning, and Carol is down there. They're calling it a home accident—injured himself lifting weights. When they slipped, his arms were pulled back. He hit his head. They could have asked a lot of other questions, but they're giving me a break. Works for me. No official stuff. We're okay there."

"How about the shit in Tucker?"

Homes dumped out portions of eggs and bacon onto two plates and slid one across to me. "I did a casual check with the office about an hour ago—overnight crimes in the area, that kind of thing. Nothing specific. No mention of anything in Tucker. As remote as that place was, they may not find anything for weeks."

"Right. And if our Cambodian friend cleans up the mess like he got rid of the body, they may not find anything at all. Wonder where he is?"

Homes opened up a beer and finished his bacon and eggs. "From what you told me, these guys don't let bygones be bygones. They keep on coming. So we need to be careful. Another thing that bothers me— how many more of these shitheads are there?"

I cleaned up my own plate, picked his up along with mine, and headed for the dishwasher. "My head is so full of other stuff, I never thought of that."

"Well, keep thinking. And watching. Now, what do we do about Dahlonega? Do we go tonight? Sunday night things should be pretty dead up there, no pun intended."

I thought about it for a minute. "First, I want to call and check on Hank. You and I can decide about going to Dahlonega. The trick is to get into that shack without being seen and then work in the dark so we don't tip off Thurlow and Uncle What's-his-name."

"Dulcie," Homes said. "Uncle Dulcie. I'm hoping he doesn't have any Cambodian relatives. I figure we go up late, park way the fuck away from the building, then walk up through the woods with a shovel and a couple of small penlights. I've got some. We do the digging as fast as we can and then get the hell out of there."

"Sounds good to me. Let's get cleaned up and get down to see Hank."

North Fulton Hospital was busy on a Sunday afternoon, when visiting hours were relaxed. Homes knew Hank's room number, but he stopped at the hospital entrance to say a few words to the security guard. They acted like old friends. Then we headed up to the third floor to see how Hank was doing. Carol was in the room and came to us as we walked in.

"God, it's good to see both of you," she said, hugging us. She looked tired and distracted. "I really can't believe this is happening."

"I can believe it," Hank said. He was wrapped up like a mummy, left arm in the air, with two black eyes, but he smiled.

"I bet you can," I said. "How is everything?"

"My left arm still hurts like hell, but they're giving me some good drugs, so things aren't a total loss."

"The kid still has a sense of humor," Homes said. "How soon do they spring you?"

"Doctor says tomorrow; maybe Tuesday," Carol said. "I'll take him home, of course. He'll have the cast on his arm for some time, but otherwise he should be able to get around. We don't want him to miss too much school."

"Sue came down earlier this morning and is contacting the school and my teachers. She doesn't know what really happened. I should be okay there." Hank shifted painfully in his bed. "Jack, Carol has filled me in from what Homes told her about what happened after we—I mean the thing in Tucker. My mind is a little cloudy about it."

"Let's just say that Homes saved both our asses."

"Balls," Homes said. "I had to drive over to Tucker anyway. I was out of beer."

Another smile from Hank made us all feel a little better.

"So what now?" Hank said.

"Homes and I were just talking about that. We figure on going back to Dahlonega tonight and seeing what we can find. If we wait until tomorrow, there may be more people around."

"Wish I could go with you," Hank said.

"Yeah, you could whack some Cambodians with your cast. You've done more than your share, kid. Take it easy for a while."

We were all silent until I felt I had to ask. "Carol, have you noticed anyone—?"

"No. No one. Nothing at all. Of course, I've been at Roxanne's most of the time. We both went back to the house to pick up some clothes for Hank and me. Nothing out of the ordinary."

"I've got your gun in the car, Carol. You ought to have it with you."

"Actually, Roxanne had two. We've been keeping them handy."

"Good," Homes said. "Hank, everything about your hospital admittance has been cleaned up, so there should be no problem there. I talked to a retired Roswell cop doing security downstairs and asked him to keep an eye on the room and you. He's going to pass that on to the other guys on duty. All he knows is that you're a friend. No false alarms, but we want to make sure you don't get any unwelcome visitors."

"I understand. Some of my buddies from school are coming down later today too."

"I stayed with Homes last night," I said, "and will probably do the same tonight. Carol, it may be late when we get back from Dahlonega. Okay if we call you?"

"I'd be upset if you didn't. And, Jack—find the gems this time." It sounded like more of an order than a request.

We said our good-byes and headed back out to Homes's truck. "Hey, it's almost dinner time," he said. "What do you say we go over to TJ's, have a couple of steaks, and try to relax? We can watch the game for a while, maybe kill some time with—what's that chick's name again?"

"Rhiannon. Her name's Rhiannon. You've known her for two or three years. Why the hell can't you remember her name?" Jerking Homes around was beginning to make me feel better.

"What the hell kind of name is Rhiannon, anyway?" he said. "Mary, I could remember. Anyway, we'll play around with her for a while and then go back to my place or head straight for Dahlonega."

"Let's do it."

TJ's had the usual Sunday football crowd in full roar when we arrived. Steelers-Bengals. Rhiannon saw us come in and found us a table. "Nice to see you boys again. Thought you forgot about me."

"How could we forget you, darlin'?" Homes said, smiling his big-daddy smile at her. "We need a Heineken, a ginger ale, and a couple of menus." She patted Homes on the head and left us.

"'How could we forget you?' You asshole, you can't even remember her name. And I'd bet real money you can't spell it."

"I need to take her out. I've been meaning to. Once I do that, I'll remember," he said.

Rhiannon came back with menus and beer. "Say, Rhiannon," Homes said. "I was just telling Jack here that I've been meaning to ask you out. What do you say we get together sometime soon?"

She laughed. "What took you so long? I thought I had bad breath."

Nothing Rhiannon had was bad. She was cute, very well built, maybe thirty. She scribbled something on the back of a napkin and handed it to Homes. "Call me. I'll have your steaks soon."

"Hey, doll," Homes said, looking at the napkin. "Are these your measurements or your phone number?"

"You're cute, copper," she said, laughing. We both watched her walk away.

"Now, that lady has a fine ass," Homes said.

"The rest of her ain't bad either," I said. We clinked our drinks and relaxed.

"Hey, just a few hours ago I wasn't sure if I was going to wind up as a sacrifice to a pissed off Buddha, and now I'm almost back to my old sinful ways," I said. "You, my friend, in addition to being a lifesaver, are a bad influence."

The crowd was into the game, but we had other things on our minds. Rhiannon brought our steaks. Homes decided not to order another beer. That was a good thing. We were on the job again. Together.

We left TJ's about seven o'clock and stopped by Homes's place before we headed north. We handled everything just as he had the night before—actually, that morning. He parked away from his usual space, and we checked the door to his apartment and then scouted all the rooms and windows when we got inside. I had to admit I liked working with him again.

"Still clean," he said, sitting on the sofa and turning on the TV. "Let's start driving up there about nine. We'll take it slow. It should be good and dark when we reach the place."

We watched a *Law and Order* rerun for maybe the fifth time. "I miss Jerry Orbach," Homes said.

"Me too. Lenny was a great philosopher."

"People think this police work is easy or that we sit around eating donuts all the time."

"Homes, you do eat donuts."

"But not all the time." He turned off the television. "Hey, Jack, tell me something. How long did we work together—two, three years?"

"Yeah, about that."

"All that time, you never told me. This Bobby Darin thing—what got you into it? I mean, Darin must have been dead when you were born."

"Just about. He died in '73. December. I was born a few years later. He was only thirty-seven when he died of some damn heart thing."

"Jesus, you even know when he died? What's the deal?"

I smiled at him. "It's because of my dad. My dad was the big fan. He had all his albums."

"But you told me you never knew your dad."

I nodded. "That's right. He was killed in Vietnam. It was just my mother and me. She kept the albums, and, when I was old enough to be interested, I started to play them. Made me feel closer to my dad, I guess. Something just clicked."

"And now you can't stop."

I laughed. "It's not that. Darin's a very misunderstood guy. A really great singer, not just the finger-snapping former rock-and-roll character. I like his moody stuff. It helps me think. And he was a good actor."

"Yeah, well, I keep hoping you'll get hooked on somebody else, buddy."

The drive to Dahlonega was uneventful. There was only one other car on the road, and it passed us. We could see a man and a woman and two kids inside. Homes had loaded a shovel in the back of his truck, and we each had a small penlight. I checked the ammunition in my Glock; it was still fully loaded. We were as ready as we could be.

We followed the same route we'd used the night before. It was just after ten when we hit the outskirts of town. "Let's drive around for a while," Homes said. "Maybe drive by the building once. See what's happening."

There was absolutely nothing going on in Dahlonega that Sunday night. Even the biker bar we passed had only two bikes outside. "I'm ready if you are," I said.

We parked his truck about a half mile from the mine and walked through the woods as much as we were able, no sounds or lights anywhere around us. As we approached the building, Homes tugged at my sleeve.

"Just for the hell of it, let's go in through the back or the side."

"Fine with me." He drew his gun, and I did the same.

There was an old entrance at the rear of the place. It took us only a minute to quietly pry the boards loose and get inside. Our penlights were just strong enough for us to observe that the place was deserted.

"You want to talk or dig?" Homes said.

I handed him the directions. "You talk, I'll dig. And let's start at the beginning and pace things off again."

We did that, with Homes running through the step thing and me carefully measuring off the number of paces. I wound up in approximately the same spot we had reached the night before, right in front of the few floor boards we had torn up, next to the large sand pile up against the back wall.

"I can't believe Don would hide the stones inside this sand pile. It doesn't make sense. So let's just start right here. I'll dig down the first forty feet," I said.

"Forty, my ass," Homes said. "Four is more like it."

I got to work, tearing up another board or two, digging as quietly as I could. The ground was a mixture of red clay and sand and wasn't too hard to get through. In about twenty minutes, I had a good-sized hole started—no gems.

"Want me to take a shift?" Homes said.

"Sure. Maybe you'll have better luck."

Homes extended the hole in all four directions and went down another foot or so. We had killed over an hour, and it was obvious we were getting nowhere.

"I think this is a lost cause, Jack," he said. "We don't even know if this is the right spot."

"I agree. And I keep waiting for visitors to show up. Let's get out of here."

Back in Homes's truck, we headed down to Roswell, both of us too pissed off to say anything.

"So what do you think?" Homes said, finally breaking the silence.

"I think we're probably way too late. The stones were probably removed some time ago."

Homes considered that for a moment. "Well, if someone did find the stones and tried to peddle them, that might have tipped somebody off. Isn't that what that guy up at UGA told you—that they could be identified?"

"Yeah. That's what he said. But maybe whoever found them is sitting on them, like Don Chambers and his crew did for all those years."

Homes hit the steering wheel with the palms of his hands. "There's too goddamned many maybes about this whole fucking thing to suit me."

We drove in silence again back to his apartment. Inside, I called Carol's cell to report. "No luck. Sorry."

"You and Homes are still alive," she said. "That's not unlucky. But I wanted you to find the gems." She sounded like she'd been drinking.

"You still at Roxie's?"

"Yes. We're watching reruns of *Jersey Shore* and drinking a little scotch."

"What the hell is *Jersey Shore*?"

"It's mind candy—something to take our minds off of what's been happening."

"How's Hank doing?"

"Fine. I left him with about a dozen of his friends from school. He was starting to look a little sleepy."

"Best thing for him. I'm at Homes's place. We're going to watch some television and call it a night. How about if we get together tomorrow and decide what to do next?"

"Good idea. Why don't you call me in the afternoon sometime?"

"Will do. Get some rest."

Homes chuckled as I hung up. "Makes me nervous thinking about those two women together."

"Yeah, it's been keeping me awake nights too." I decided not to tell him about the movie and walked over and got a beer from his fridge and tossed it to him.

"Either one of them is probably just as dangerous as those Cambodians."

I laughed. "You have a point. So how come I'm not afraid?"

"Because you're stupid, stupid," he said. "Speaking of our friend the Cambodian—what did you call him?"

"Prum."

"Yeah, Prum. So where the fuck is he?"

"Hey, you're the cop. You tell me."

Homes thought a minute. "We're in kind of a bad position here. I can ask my people to call the Tucker cops and have him picked up, or at least look for him. Trouble is, I don't have a legit reason. I can't start telling everyone about jewels and headless corpses and murders. Besides, my money says that guy is in hiding. I figure he does that pretty good."

"You're right. So what do we do?"

"I can do this. I'll ask the Tucker cops to look for him as a person of interest in some fake robbery thing. That might turn up something."

"Homes, my guess is that he'll stay hidden and then come after one or all of us. That's what they do, this crazy sect he belongs to, according to Dr. Chang at UGA and my own study on the Internet. These gems are a big fucking religious deal to them, and they'll kill themselves—and us—to get them back. Even if Prum is the last one of his kind close by—and we don't know that—sooner or later they'll just send more of them."

"If that's the case, we need a permanent solution. Like this." Homes pulled out his weapon and placed it on the coffee table in front of us. "We need to find him before he finds us."

"Right. But my feeling is that he'll find us first."

"So what's your move tomorrow?"

I took a deep breath. "I need to go by the office and do a couple of things, then check in on Hank, then head for Carol's to discuss the situation."

Homes drained his beer, picked up his weapon, and smiled. "Just don't leave all your good, hard detective work between the sheets, buddy. If this Prum guy shows up at Carol's, you're going to need to be on top of your game, not hers. And take this with you." He handed me his gun.

"I've got my Glock."

"And this baby makes two. You may need a throw-down, and I've got extras."

"Okay. It can't hurt. I want to be ready for that bastard. He got hold of me once, and it wasn't any fun."

Homes stood and stretched. "I'm going into the office fairly early in the morning. How about if I check up on you every hour? I'll call your cell. If I get no answer, I call out the militia. You can call me first to let me know things are okay. Sleep in as late as you want. I'll check with you later."

I woke up shortly after eight, showered, and headed for the office, setting Homes's alarm system before I left his apartment. I needed clean clothes but figured that could wait for a while. The truth was that going straight to my apartment made me feel uncomfortable. Bad memories. And I didn't want to deal with Prum if he was there. I got some coffee and a donut on the way.

Instead of walking straight into the office, I checked the locked door. No obvious marks. All appeared to be calm inside. I pulled my weapon and unlocked the door as quietly as I could. My office isn't large, and a quick glance around made me feel better. I closed and locked the door and decided to check the outside of the safe the same way. I found no marks or scratches. I called Homes to check in and then called the hospital for an update on Hank. Everything was cool.

I spent the next hour adding to my notes on the case and thinking things through. One of the few positives was that the whole case—especially recent events—had taken my mind off drinking, at least temporarily. I hadn't gone off on a real binge either—the lost-weekend kind of thing. It made me smile to think a murderous Cambodian thug had pulled off that trick. Of course, he had almost killed me. Twice. Not exactly one of AA's recommended twelve steps to stop drinking. I went over to my safe, opened it, and took out the small sack of gems Hank had given me, spreading them on top of my desk. No doubt they were beautiful. I wondered how many people had been killed—and were still being killed—for them over the years. Maybe centuries. I wanted to wrap this case up soon without adding to the number. The gems went back in the safe.

I thought it was Carol when my phone rang, but it was Hank.

"Jack! Jack, I've got it!"

The kid was really wound up. "Hank, take it easy."

"Jack, it's not Dahlonega. It's the house. They're at home!"

"What's at home?"

"The gems are right at home. I know they are. I had a dream—I should have known."

"What dream? What the hell are you talking about? Maybe those drugs—"

"Jack, what Dad said in that diary—the last thing—something about remembering what we did when it was all over."

"Yeah, you said you went gem mining."

"Sometimes. But the last thing we did—Jack, it's so simple—the last thing we did was go home. That's what he said in the note. He even repeated it. *'Home is the most important thing.'*" Hank was shouting.

"Calm down, Hank. Of course you went home. So what?"

"Don't you see? We were trying to complicate things. Thinking too hard. Dad was keeping it simple. He hid the gems at home, I know he did. The instructions—"

"What about them?"

"I couldn't remember them exactly from the other night, but I think if you start at our front door, they'll take you through the house and into the backyard. I'm positive."

I wanted to tell him he'd been positive about Dahlonega and the gem mine, too, but I kept my mouth shut.

"Okay, okay. Take it easy. I'm going out to see Carol in a little while, and I'll give it a shot. What have we got to lose?"

"This is it, Jack. I know it is."

"Okay. Try to get some rest. When are you getting out?"

"They tell me tomorrow, but I don't want you to wait that long."

"I'll call Carol right now and tell her I'm on my way. Then we'll let you know."

As skeptical as I was, I had to admit the kid had begun to cheer me up. If we couldn't deal with Prum, maybe we could at least find the damned gems. What happened after that was anyone's guess, but I started daydreaming again about millions of dollars. And Carol. And occasionally Roxanne. Or both. Hey, I was beginning to feel normal again, at least normal for me.

Carol was watching for my car and opened the door as I drove up. There was something about her that didn't look right. Usually immaculately groomed, she looked rumpled; her hair was disheveled, no makeup, no jewelry. As we stepped inside, she pressed the security system alarm, put her arms around my neck, and we moved up against each other, mouths locked together. It was obvious she'd been drinking. She moaned and moved her hands up and down my ass, and I moved my hands to her breasts. This was a lot more aggressive than she had ever been before. For a minute, I thought I was with Roxanne. Then I got a good look at her eyes, so dilated I could scarcely see her pupils. There was something going on.

"I want to fuck, Jack." She formed her words slowly and carefully, right out of a Roxanne script. I had never heard her use that kind of language before.

"I can tell. Why don't we sit down first, and I'll tell you why Hank is all excited."

She frowned but took my hand and walked unsteadily into the great room here the bar was.

"I want a drink," she said. "A big one. You know what I like." She sat down on the large sofa and smiled a lopsided smile at me. I walked to the bar, mixed her a very light drink, and sat down next to her.

"We've done it here before," she said, stretching out on the sofa and reaching for me. "Don and I used to do it here, too. And over there on the rug. Everywhere."

"Let's take it a little easy, Carol. I want to explain what Hank has come up with. We may need to do a little work afterwards. It's important."

Another frown. "What could be more important than this?" she said, unbuttoning her blouse.

High or not, Carol was one of the most beautiful women I had ever seen, and I was tempted to put off Hank's suggestion for a while, anyway. But something was bothering me, and it wasn't just Carol's strange behavior.

"It's about the jewels, Carol."

She sat up immediately. "Why the fuck didn't you say so? Do you have them? Give them to me." She didn't try to button her open blouse.

I looked at her and wondered again what was going on. This Carol was a completely different person. "No. Not yet. Hank says he had a revelation and knows—"

She waved her hand in the air. "Hank doesn't know shit. He's already sent us on one wild goose chase to Dahlonega." She forced a laugh. "Roxanne thinks he's gay." She picked up her drink and drained it.

"He thinks the gems are here. Right here."

"My God. In the house? But I've looked all—" She waved both arms in the air. "All over the fucking place."

"I know you have. Hank feels that his father—Don's—hint in that little diary we read wasn't about Dahlonega at all. He thinks it was about this house. He thinks the gems are probably buried outside somewhere. Anyway, that's his idea."

Carol faked another laugh. "That's just bullshit. How does he know? It's more time wasted. I want another drink." She held out her glass.

"Tell you what. This won't take long. Let's spend a few minutes checking out Hank's idea, and then we can have as many drinks as we want."

"*I don't want to wait!*" she shouted. "I've been waiting for over two years. I don't have Don. I don't have those goddamned jewels." She threw her glass across the room, against the bar. Pieces shattered all over.

"Carol, I need your help to do this, and you need to be able to focus. I need a shovel, and you'll need to read—"

"Read? Read what?"

"The directions, or instructions, or whatever the hell they are that the monk in Tucker translated for me."

"What monk? Oh, that bastard—the one you talked to?"

"That's right." I reached into my pants pocket and handed her the notes. "Here."

"What the fuck is this?" she said, reading the papers. "This doesn't make any sense."

"That's the English translation of Don's Cambodian notes. They're instructions for finding something—maybe the gems."

"But this doesn't really tell us anything—where to start or stop or what to do. It's another dead end."

"It may be. In Dahlonega, we just started at the front door of this shack, paced off the steps, pried up some floor boards, and started digging."

"Great. Just great. So now you want to dig up my house. You're really a shitty detective, Jack. Where's my glass?" She looked around the sofa and table.

I was getting pretty mad by now. "You smashed it against the bar. Look, we can either take a few minutes to check this out or we can forget about the gems completely. I don't care anymore."

She stood up and looked down at me. I'd never seen a look like that on her before—complete disgust.

"If you forget about the gems, you can forget about me too. There's a shovel in the shed outside." She motioned for me to follow her, and we both headed in that direction. I kicked a few pieces of broken glass out of the way as we crossed the large room. Carol half-buttoned her blouse as we walked. Coming back inside, I called Homes to check in and tell him I was okay for the night, although the way things were going, it didn't look like there would be much of a night. He wanted to talk, but I told him we were on another scavenger hunt and I'd update him soon. Then we walked up to the front door. I turned toward Carol.

"Okay, you start reading the notes, and I'll pace the steps off." I didn't know how well she was going to do, but she started to read, and I assumed a normal pace for each step. The directions headed me down the same side hallway we had just used to go out to the shed.

"You think he hid the gems in the shed?" I asked.

"How the fuck should I know? There's a lot more writing here." She continued reading.

Her directions moved me past the shed, into the backyard. It was huge and lushly landscaped. Trees and flowers of every variety surrounded the home. *Great.* It would take a year to find anything in this botanical jungle.

"Here's the end of this shit," she said, reading the last line. "This is ridiculous."

I paced it off carefully and stopped more or less in front of a pretty shrub that was unlike any other in the garden. It had a mixture of bright yellow flowers and shiny black berries surrounded by red petals.

"Oh, that's Mickey," she said, "Don's favorite fucking bush. It's supposed to be Vietnamese. He ordered it from a nursery in South Florida that guaranteed it wouldn't die. And it never did. Only Don died. See, that's a joke. Don's dead and the bush is alive and I'm alone."

I ignored her and checked the base of the plant. "Why Mickey?"

"He always said the flowers resembled Mickey Mouse's face, but I never could see it. He said the plant was supposed to bring good luck. That's another big fucking joke. There should be a tag with a name somewhere ..."

I found it and read *Ochna integerrima*. "I can't even pronounce this thing."

"Neither can I. Who needs a goddamned Vietnamese plant anyway? I told him I wasn't even born when Vietnam was over. I hate Vietnam. I hate this whole ..." Her voice drifted off.

"I don't want to dig it up and kill it. It's a pretty bush."

"Digging that damn thing up won't hurt it. Don was afraid it was dying a couple of times, so he transplanted it all—"

She dropped the notes and brought her hands to her face. "Oh, my God. He was constantly digging up that plant and moving it. I never thought anything about it. But now—"

"Well, maybe we've got something," I said. I looked around the huge yard. There was plenty of room for someone to hide, even in broad daylight. I pulled up my pants leg, reached down to my ankle, and pulled Homes's drop gun from the sweatband that held it in place. I was going to give it to Carol while I dug, but in her condition that would be stupid. I laid it down beside the plant, in easy reach.

"What's that for?" she said.

"That's for any grim-looking Asian guys who might show up."

I started to dig, trying to keep the plant's roots intact. I hadn't been at it five minutes when I hit something.

"Probably just a rock," Carol said. "Don said this soil was full of them."

I felt around with the shovel. What it was hitting was metal, or sounded like it. I cleared more of the dirt and finally saw a long, rusty metal container. It looked like an old ammunition box from my army days.

"Does this look familiar?"

"I've never seen it before." Carol bent over me as I dug under the box. I tipped it up enough so I could bring it to the surface. I had only dug down about two feet.

"These ammunition boxes have a clamp on each side but no separate lock. What do you say we go back inside to open it up? I'd feel a lot safer."

"Give me the goddamned box!" she said, pulling it from my hands. "It's mine. And what's inside is mine."

"It's pretty heavy," I said.

"Jewels are never that heavy," she said, shaking the container. It sounded like it was full of gravel.

Inside the house, Carol rearmed the security system. Her concentration seemed to be improving. I replaced Homes's gun in the sweatband around my ankle.

"Let's take the box into Don's office," she said. She set it down on the desk, and I reached over to flip the clamps. The ammunition box was for .50-caliber shells, probably World War II surplus, easily purchased at any army surplus store. It was about eight inches long, six inches high, and maybe five inches deep. *Plenty of room for a lot of something.*

"Here goes."

When I pulled the collapsible handle on top and opened the box, I couldn't help gasping. It was the biggest collection of precious gems I had ever seen.

"Jesus," she said, "there must be a hundred stones here." Her eyes were wide.

"Or more." Most of the gems were smaller than the four I had in the pouch in my office safe. Primarily emeralds and rubies and some other rough stones I couldn't identify. They shimmered like a thousand lasers in the light from the desk lamp.

Carol dug into the box, pulled out two handfuls of gems, and rubbed them on her arms. "At last. My God, I wonder what they're worth," she said. She continued digging and rubbing.

"They're worth your life, Carol. They were worth Don's and almost Hank's and mine. And Tim Tomlin's. Let's not forget those monks in Cambodia. No telling how many others."

"I don't care about them. Any of them. These are so fucking beautiful."

She had the strangest smile on her face as she picked the box up and walked over to a large glass bowl on a shelf in the office. She poured about half the stones into it. She walked back toward me carrying the bowl. As she came closer, I could see her eyes were dark and still dilated. She was breathing faster. "Let's go upstairs, Jack."

"Are you sure? We ought to—"

"I want to fuck with these stones, Jack. Now. I want to throw them on the bed and just fuck. You can come up with me, or I'll do it all by myself. It doesn't matter to me." She turned and headed for the staircase. I followed.

In the bedroom, she turned the bowl over and spilled the gems onto her bed. Then she slipped off her clothes and laid down on the stones. She held her arms out for me. "You know you want me."

"Carol, these are raw, unpolished, stones. They're ragged and sharp. They can cut and hurt."

"I don't care about the pain. I like pain, Jack. Didn't I tell you?" She was breathing heavily.

"Let's put the gems on the floor," I said. "They'll be right underneath us."

"Not underneath us, stupid. I want us on top of them. I can call someone else if you're not interested."

That did it. "Carol, you know I'm interested. Just stop this shit and pull yourself together. I know you're on something. I don't care what it is. If you want to make love, let's clear these things off and—"

"Make love? What a laugh. You're all the same, you men. All the same. I'm not interested in love, Jack. It came close to love with Don, but not even with him. I want to do it on these gems, Jack. I don't care if they bruise and cut us. I want to feel that pain. Then I'll know this was all worth it."

"This isn't the way, Carol. This isn't—"

"It's *my* way, goddammit. *My way!* If you don't want me, then get out. *Get out!*"

There was no saving the situation. I turned from her and headed out of the bedroom.

"No. Wait," she said. "I have something to say to you."

"There isn't anything else you can say. You have what you want. I'm leaving."

She did another version of that phony, forced laugh. "No, I want you to hear this." She rubbed her hands over the gems. "Last night. At Roxanne's. We were drinking and fooling around. She gave me something—a couple of those pills of hers. I hadn't had anything in so long. It felt good. We were watching television on her bed. She started kissing me and I—I kissed her back. Everything happened so slowly." The weird smile was back on her face. "Before I knew it, she was on top of me, and we were doing it. Roxanne knows about pain, Jack, and how to make it feel good."

"I don't want to hear this—"

"Let me finish. I liked it, Jack. I liked it a lot. I finally let go of the pressure. It's been a long time. I've—been with women before. Lots of women. If I call her now, she'll be over in a minute." She looked directly at me.

"Then call her," I said and walked out of the room, out of the house, and into my car.

It was close to midnight when I pulled into my complex, already half-asleep. I couldn't believe what I'd just gone through with Carol. But she had her gems now. As far as I was concerned, the job was done.

As I stepped out of my car, a well-muscled arm wrapped around my neck, and I felt a familiar knife blade at my throat. Prum was back.

He quickly grabbed the gun from my arm holster and then pushed me around to the passenger side. He opened the door and, knife jabbing at my throat, made me slide across to the driver's position again. "You drive Tucker. You make trick, I kill you, then kill woman and boy."

I was going to tell him he needed a new routine but figured he wouldn't be amused. "No stone," I said. "No have stone."

"You talk in Tucker," he said. "I make you tell."

He threw my gun in the backseat and kept the knife at my neck. "Gun for coward," he said. "No honor."

I was glad I had strapped Homes's throwaway to my right ankle before I left Carol's. Since I hadn't had it on me the first time Prum went through this routine, I figured I had at least a chance of getting to it at some point. There was little chance Homes would call my place as he had before and realize something was wrong. When I called him from Carol's, I said I would be there the rest of the night. I was on my own.

Something strange started happening to me then. I should have been terrified or at least frightened. After all, this guy was planning to torture and kill me. But I wasn't. Instead, I was beginning to get mad. Really mad.

"What did you do with the other man?" I asked him. I had nothing to lose by talking.

"Other man gone. Soon you be gone. Sacred stone be back in temple."

"Why not kill me here? Why Tucker? I'm getting tired of Tucker." I sounded punchy.

"You my sacrifice at altar of Devadatta Buddha in Tucker. Then I find stone. All die."

One-track mind. I decided I'd had enough of this conversation and kept my mouth shut until we reached his place.

"You park in back barn."

I pulled into almost the same area my car had been in before. Now I was starting to get scared again. This was close to being the end. I remembered Prum's muscled body. There was no way I could out-wrestle him, even at the top of my game, and I was at rock-bottom now. And he was an expert with that knife. Something would have to work in my favor so I could reach my weapon.

"You come here," he said, opening the passenger side door and motioning me to follow him. I thought this might be the right time to try for the gun at my ankle, but Prum seemed to sense I had something on my mind. He extended the knife, watching me closely. He pushed me toward the main door to the barn, his knife pressed against my back. "You open." We walked inside, and he flipped a wall switch. Several small lights came on, one directly above that repulsive Buddha. He pushed me toward a chair. "Sit." I prayed he wouldn't tie my hands behind me; he was too eager for the finish.

He backed slowly toward the Buddha, knife in hand, watching me intently. Then he tucked the knife in the belt on his waist, reached back, and picked up the long, golden sword I had seen before. He walked toward me.

"You tell where stone."

I shrugged and thought about smiling to show I wasn't afraid. But there was no playing with this guy. "I don't have stone. I don't know."

"You lie," he said, almost screaming the words. "If you not have, woman and boy have. I kill you. They talk. I kill them. All die."

He motioned with the sword for me to stand up and move toward the Buddha.

"On knees before Devadatta," he screamed. "On knees for offering."

I was fairly calm, considering. Kneeling down would actually give me better leverage to grab the gun at my ankle, but I would have to be fast, and I would only have one chance. I knelt down. He began chanting something. I felt him come closer. *This is it.*

My right arm reached for the pistol and grabbed it as I fell toward my right. I felt the swoosh from his sword just missing me as I turned on my side and fired. I hit Prum squarely in the chest. I saw the hatred in his eyes. I waited for him to fall, but he turned slightly toward me and raised the sword over his head again.

Impossible! That shot had hit him cleanly. Close to the heart, if not through it. I thought, *What if the bastard doesn't have a heart?* I fired again. He staggered slightly but kept coming. Just what I needed—a fucking Cambodian Superman. On my back, I took careful aim at his eyes and fired once more. A small round black hole appeared just over his right eyebrow. He fell slowly to his knees, hands still wrapped around the sword, staring sightlessly at me. He stayed that way, almost like he was praying.

For a moment I thought he was still alive. The anger I'd been feeling welled up, and I felt like shooting him again. One more for Hank, another for Tim Tomlin, and a third for Don Chambers. Instead, I got to my feet, walked up to him, and kicked his body over. He'd had three chances at me. *Fuck him, his sword, and his sacrifice.*

21.

remembered what Homes had said the last time about cleaning up, but I hadn't touched anything other than the door to the barn, so I wiped the handle quickly. I would take the throwaway back to Homes and let him deal with it. There was nothing else to tie me to the scene or to Prum. I thought about burning that place down, along with its evil Buddha, but that would only attract attention. I guessed it would be a while before somebody found him, and that was fine with me. I drove back to Roswell slowly, the adrenalin kick starting to fade. It had been quite a night. I dragged myself into the apartment, reset the alarm, and collapsed on my bed. The last thing I remember thinking was, *What if there are more of these assholes?*

Carol's call woke me about ten thirty. Her voice was strained.

"Have a good night's sleep?" she said.

"Not really. I don't need any more nights like that one."

She was silent for a moment. "Are you coming out?"

"I think you fired me last night."

"I—I did nothing of the kind. Hank's here. He's expecting you. I can make some brunch."

For the first time, I didn't want anything from her. "I'm not hungry, but I'll be out in about an hour." I made a quick call to Homes to let him know I was okay and told him I'd had another adventure in Tucker and we needed to talk. He wanted me to come over right away, but I said I was headed back to Carol's and would see him later.

After cleaning up, I made a brief stop at the office, picked up the four stones in the pouch in my safe, and then headed straight for Camelot, Glock under my arm. There was only light traffic on the way to Carol's, and I found myself checking the rear view mirror purely out of habit. After the past week's events, I wondered if I would ever feel comfortable again.

Carol was at the front door. She said nothing to me as we walked into the great room. Her eyes looked clear, and she was dressed immaculately. Hank was in the single chair, left arm in a cast, elevated a little but not as much as when he was in the hospital.

"Good to see you, Hank. Your arm looks like it's been adjusted a little."

"Yeah, they made me a little more comfortable before I left. The right arm is at least workable." He moved it slowly to show me. "Sue is going to get me to class. I ought to be able to drive in about a month—earlier if I can stick my arm out the window."

"Don't make that too soon, Hank," Carol said. "Why don't you two come in the kitchen and have something to eat."

I wanted to pass on the food just to spite her, but I was ravenous. I had seconds of everything. Hank had already gone in to see the gems and was as impressed as we were.

"I've never seen anything like them," he said.

"Well, if it wasn't for you, we never would have seen them at all," I said.

Then I told them about last night and my latest adventure with Prum. Carol looked down at the table as I spoke and never met my eyes. Hank just shook his head.

"Not again, Jack. I can't believe it. When will this shit be over?"

"I don't know if it ever will, Hank. My guess is that the only chance we have is to get those gems back where they belong."

"They *are* where they belong, dammit. The gems belong to me." Carol's voice was loud and strident. "They were Don's and now they're mine. They're all I ever wanted." It was a replay from last night. Hank and I looked at her in disbelief.

"Carol, you can't be serious," he said.

"I can and I am. The gems are Don's legacy. And mine. Jack, if you were doing your job, you'd have some connections that could help us find a way to sell them. If not, I'll find someone else. They've got to be worth millions. Millions." Her eyes had a far-off look. Her fists were tightly clenched. "Of course, I'll keep a few."

Hank looked at her as if she was crazy. "Carol, if those gems don't go back, you'll be in danger for the rest of your life. You didn't hear Dr. Chang's explanation of this cult and their history. They never stop coming. Look what happened to Jack last night."

Carol stood up quickly, knocking her chair to the floor. "I don't give a shit about Chang or anyone else. I want these stones. I'll find someone to protect me. I always have." She turned and left the room.

"Jack, what the hell is going on with her?"

"Damned if I know. It started last night before I left. Hank, we can't let her do this."

"How can we stop her—take the stones by force? Legally—"

"There is no *legally*. There's nothing legal about any of what's happened, from the time your dad took them out of the jungle right up to my shooting Prum last night. The whole thing is illegal and immoral, dammit." The sound of my voice surprised even me.

"What do you know about immoral?" It was Carol, standing at the edge of the kitchen.

"Immoral is being raped at the age of fifteen by your own father, on the street by sixteen, fucking in the big city just to survive. Making money every sickening way imaginable. Taking drugs to make yourself numb enough to keep doing it. That's immoral. I vowed to get out of all of that and never have to worry about money again. Don gave me protection and a way out, and he wanted me to have those goddamned gems. Now I'll never let them go."

She became hysterical, and I stood up and reached for her. She pulled away from me.

"It's okay, Carol. You know you don't need those damn jewels. Don made sure you and Hank would be okay. You have plenty of money. You'll be fine without them. With them, you'll be in danger for the rest of your life."

When she calmed down, we all walked into Don's office. Carol opened the safe and took out the ammunition box. She placed it on the table and looked up at us.

"One more time," she said, opening the box. She stared at the gems for a minute and then plunged her hands deeply into the box. After a minute, she pulled her hands out and rubbed them on her shorts. "All right. Take them. I don't care. Take them."

"What are you going to do with them, Jack?"

"I thought about it on the way over here," I said. "I'm going to take them to Brother Samrin at the temple in Tucker and ask him for help. I don't know what else to do. Going to the FBI at this stage and telling them the story will eventually tie in the murders of the two Cambodians. It could send me to prison and maybe destroy Homes's career. That's just unnecessary."

Carol walked over to the window and stared outside.

"That sounds like a plan to me. Carol, what do you think?" Hank said.

She said nothing and continued to stand by the window. I went to her and put a hand on her shoulder. "I'm going to drive to Tucker right now and get this over with. I'll call you later." She pulled away from my hand. I told Hank I'd be talking to him and left the house. Back in my car, I called Homes and said I'd like his company on the trip to Tucker. He said he'd take the rest of the day off. I drove by the station to pick him up. I started to tell him the full story about Prum, but he interrupted.

"You know, Jack," he said as we drove, "you keep driving to Tucker like this, three or four times a day, and you might learn to like the place and take up farming." He poked me in the ribs.

"Sorry I'm not in a laughing mood, Homes. It was a bad night all around."

"I can imagine—with that Prum character."

"There's more to it than that." I told him what happened with Carol and then the whole Prum adventure and thanked him for giving me the throwaway. "You saved my life. Again."

He laughed. "The amount of beer you owe me is going to keep me on my ass for some time," he said. "I don't get the routine with Carol," he said. "I thought you two were getting close."

"So did I. There's no question she was high on something, but she was bitter as hell, and I hadn't given her any reason to be." I didn't want to tell him about Carol and Roxanne together.

"I told you there was something going on with that chick, partner. Sorry it turned out badly."

We reached the temple and drove into the parking lot. "Nice-looking place, if you like creepy Asian shit," Homes said.

"Actually, it's not creepy at all—not compared to that stuff we saw in the barn." I lifted the box of gems from the backseat and walked over to the main entrance. I rang the chimes. A different, younger monk opened the door. "I'd like to see Brother Samrin," I said. "Please tell him that Mr. Novak is here asking for his help."

The monk bowed, closed the door, and was back in a minute. "Please enter."

He walked us back to Samrin's office, knocked, and then left quietly.

"Come in."

Samrin was seated behind his desk, looking grim. He did not stand or offer us a chair.

"I have to say I am not pleased to see you again, Mr. Novak." He looked carefully at Homes in his uniform. "I see you have brought the police with you."

"I'm not here in any official capacity," Homes said. "I'm simply a friend of Jack's—Mr. Novak's."

"I see." Samrin appeared to consider this for a moment. "Please sit down."

I put the box on the floor, took a deep breath, and began. "Brother Samrin, I have to tell you a rather long story. It's necessary to explain what has happened and why I'm here. I'm in serious trouble, as are many of my friends, and I need your help."

He waved a hand but said nothing. I told him the entire story, leaving out only the parts about shooting the two Cambodians. Though that was entirely self-defense, I didn't think it would help our situation. His eyes widened at several points, but he never said a word. Finally, I stopped talking, reached down, and lifted the box to my lap.

"I have the stones here and, if it is possible, I would like you to return them to their rightful home. I realize this may place you in some danger. I will leave and take them with me if that is what you prefer."

Samrin stared at both of us for some time. "And if I do ask you to leave, Mr. Novak, what will you do then?"

I shook my head. "I don't know. I've never believed in curses before, but this whole situation has changed my mind. I just don't think this will end until these gems are returned."

Samrin stood and walked around his desk to the largest statue of Buddha in his office. He stood before it for several minutes. "I have devoted my life to my faith and to nonviolence, Mr. Novak, following the true path of Buddha. I have never understood the Ikko-Ikki and their savage ways. They do not follow the true path. They worship the false Devadatta Buddha, and they are evil." He returned to his desk and sat down.

"It is possible that I can return these stones to the Ikko-Ikki in Cambodia. It will not be easy, but it can be done. However, I cannot guarantee that the Ikko-Ikki will leave your lives alone. There are some people here who—" He stopped for a moment and changed his mind about something. "I will do this, Mr. Novak. Not for you or your friends, but because it may help to restore harmony and serenity where they have not existed for some time. That would be the wish of the divine Buddha."

He stood and rang a small bell. The younger monk reappeared. I turned to say something to Samrin, but he had his back to us. I placed the box on the floor, and we followed the other monk down the corridor and out of the temple.

"Now, that's a man who has it together," Homes said. I agreed.

On the ride back, I was distracted, thinking about Carol. It wasn't until we were almost in Roswell that I remembered the little sack of four gems still in my jacket pocket.

22.

It was close to midnight as we approached the dilapidated gem mine shack in Dahlonega. This was beginning to feel like an old, familiar routine.

"You know, you could have just thrown these fucking things in the Chattahoochee River, Jack," Homes said, playing with the small sack of gems.

"I know, I know. There's just something about leaving them in this phony gem mine that makes sense to me. Poetic, maybe."

"I don't know a hell of a lot about poetry," Homes said. "Why not take them back to Samrin?"

"Something told me we had outlived our welcome there, and I wasn't about to stir that whole thing up again." We went in through the back way, penlights in hand. We walked to the rear of the old mine and stood in front of the huge pile of sand. I opened the sack and spilled the gems out into my hand.

"Want to throw a couple in?" I asked Homes.

"Uh, I'm not superstitious, Jack, but if it's all the same to you, I'd rather not touch those little fuckers."

I grinned and picked up one of the broken boards on the floor. I used it to dig several holes in the sand pile, and then I threw the stones into them as hard as I could. I raked the board back and forth over the top of the pile until enough sand had fallen down to cover the area where I'd been working. Finally, we left the place.

We drove back to Roswell in Homes's truck. He pulled over and looked at me. "You know, Jack, I've got the perfect ending to this case."

"What's that?"

"You and I retire and come back up here and open up an ice cream store in Dahlonega. I know an old gem mine we can get—cheap. You can sit on a stool dishing out ice cream to the kids while you listen to Bobby Darin. We can even get Uncle Dulcie to work weekends for us. What do you think?"

"I think we both need a rest, buddy."

23.

The next morning I woke up earlier than I expected and, for the first time in quite a while, made my own breakfast. I ate slowly, drank several cups of coffee, and thought over the events of the past week. I wondered if Samrin could get the stones back to Cambodia and the Temple of the Devadatta Buddha. And if so, how would the Cambodian monks over there react? Would I still have those crazy bastards tracking me for the rest of my life? Or was it over?

I forced myself to take stock of my personal situation. I had met a beautiful but troubled woman and almost been killed several times. For what? Sex? Absolutely. Money? Maybe. And now, what did I have? I couldn't get what had happened with Carol the previous night out of my mind and the look in her eyes when she saw the gems. That may have finished it between us, but I had to admit I didn't want it to end. And her relationship with Roxanne was both troubling and provocative. Troubling because I didn't know what it meant for the future. Provocative because ... well, just provocative. I decided I needed a little time to myself to think through everything that had happened. Just to be safe, I reset the alarm as I left the apartment.

Back in my office, I went over to the safe, put my Glock and holster back inside, locked it, and went to the desk and turned on the computer. As I watched it boot up, I shook my head. I walked back to the safe, unlocked it, and strapped on the Glock again. *Why be stupid?* I'd probably be doing that for a while.

My message light had been blinking, but I chose to ignore it. Now I took a deep breath, pressed the button, and heard Carol's voice.

"Jack, I did a lot of thinking after you left yesterday. I suppose I owe you an apology for my attitude and actions. I can't explain them, except to say that there are a lot of things in my past that I thought I had buried for good. Don helped me with that. He was a positive force in my life that's gone now and will never be back. I thought you might be—I'm sorry. You're a nice guy. I went over to Roxanne's last night and stayed there. We talked about a lot of things. We decided to—Jack, we're going to spend some time together in Europe, leaving later this week. Visiting places we've never been to or want to see again."

She stopped speaking for a moment, and I could hear her breathing softly. "Please don't take this the wrong way. I don't want you to call. I don't know when I'll be back or—anything. Thanks."

I listened to the hum from the recorder after she hung up. Strangely, I felt no emotion at all. I wanted to feel loss or anger. But nothing.

I should have called Father Tom and talked this whole thing out. Homes was my best friend, and he helped every way he could, but it was different with Father Tom. Maybe it was that old Catholicism thing I was feeling. Instead, I ignored it and went to a movie, something nominated for an Academy Award that made no sense. It kept me from thinking for a while. It was about seven o'clock when I got out. I decided to head to Mucky McCarthy's and talk to Erin Doyle. She was a good listener and always helped to clear my mind. I wasn't thinking about sex—a rarity for me. I just wanted to talk.

It was still early at Mucky's. Only one other guy was at the bar. A few people were having dinner. I thought I might have the fish and chips or take Erin to dinner someplace. I would apologize for the other night. I remembered the man behind the bar from my last visit. Erin had called him Sean.

He came up to me, and I had to force myself to order a ginger ale. "Boss lady around, Sean?"

Sean smiled as he brought the drink and placed it in front of me. "Not likely. At least not for some time."

"Out of town?" I took a sip.

"You could say that, mate. She's on her honeymoon. Got married in Ireland a couple of days ago." He walked over to his other customer as I stared at his back. When he came toward me again, I said, "I didn't know she was engaged." The truth was I had never taken time to notice if she was wearing a ring or not. As usual, I was only interested in what I wanted.

"Oh, yeah," he said. "For several months now. Nice guy. A lawyer. Not Irish, but nice." He smiled and walked away from me.

I felt it this time. All of it: Erin, Carol, Roxanne, the gems, Prum. I felt it deep and long and hard. That's when I ordered my first one.

They closed the place around two, after I had tried to drink all of their Jameson and destroy all of their furniture. They said I kept screaming about Bobby Darin being my father. That's when they called Homes to pick me up and take me home.

ABOUT THE AUTHOR

Reg Ivory served seven years as a B-52 navigator-bombardier in the US Air Force, where he won eleven Air Medals. He has been a newspaper industry lobbyist and director of the Southern Newspaper Publishers Association. He is also the author of the political thriller *There is No President*. He lives with his wife, Cathy, in Nashville, Tennessee.